LE MARQUIS DE FOLIE

BY
SHANE SPARKES

ISBN-13: 978-0-9979522-2-3
Library of Congress Control Number: 2017930468
Psychologiko Books, Altadena, CALIFORNIA

PsychoLogiko Books
P.O. Box 4211
Burbank, CA 91503

CHAPTER ONE

I

I am a psychotherapist. This means that I am diseased. I won't ask your forgiveness for stating this. It is the truth, this proposition. All psychotherapists are sick. However, that doesn't mean that becoming a psychotherapist is what caused my sickness. Perhaps I have always been ill. Perhaps I have always harbored a germ. Perhaps it was suspended and aloof for a while before naturally locating its pistil, which took time, nourishment, and the right contingencies to develop. Either way, I am here now. I am a psychotherapist. I am diseased.

I am one of those horribly two-faced people. I spend my life smiling and laughing when inside I am evil. If you think that my story is going to be one of redemption or recovery, or that I am going to 'arc' and shift in my disposition, for the better, or really in any way, then this general hypothesis would be misconstrued. There will be no movement here—there won't even be paralysis—if that makes any sense. There will only be dull whimpers of a disgraceful entity masquerading as self-reflection. Forever will I rebel against Aristotle's *Poetics*.

Already I digress. I am tangential, circumstantial. My thought process is admirable only in its faux formality. Yes, two-faced. I am two-faced. How should I characterize this?

I am floridly psychotic. I am not speaking of psychotic in the common sense of the word, where an individual, for an unknown reason indefatigable in its perplexity, is unable to attain an emotional or spiritual transposition with another human being and cares little about exploiting and destroying them. This too is an interesting phenomenon. Altogether, I cannot say that I am not touched by it. However, when I say that I am psychotic, firstly, I mean to say that I am detached. My consciousness is too heavy and obtuse for the world.

Even as I write this, the strange sensation of self-loathing becomes me.

I am from that detestable breed of dog that listens to a client but hears what some other force wishes them to hear. I had a young woman come in for help. She was crying. Her filthy and tussled hair aggravated her portly visage. The litany of green and purple bruises on her arms, swirling like gangrenous nebulae around what seemed to be infected puncture wounds from someone else's needle, appeared like abstract splotches on a pallid vellum canvas. Her affect was quite labile for the dead.

She wanted me to soothe her like some surrogate father or lover. I knew this because of the way she looked at me, all downtrodden and besotted, like a little girl whom had been muddied and scraped her knee. So, I treated her like a little girl. I spoke softly. I leaned in. My eyes, I am certain, emitted some kind of warmth. I offered her encouragement. "You'll be ok. This is just a trip, your relapse," I said. "Stumbles are a part of the recovery process."

She smiled, so hopeful and picturesque in her mania. She said she felt better. Her symptoms had diminished by the end of the session she said after I prompted her response. I believed her. I didn't believe her. Really, I believed in the memory that was most easily invested. We made plans to talk again soon. My job was done. I was proud of myself.

Three days later I received the call. She had been hospital-ized by an emergency psychiatric team, whom had been contacted by the police, whom in turn had been contacted by her eight-year-old son via emergency. Mommy fell down and was having trouble breathing, he said. He was clueless, like me. She had failed at killing herself just like she had failed at everything else.

"How am I going to have to explain this to the Department of Mental Health?" is what I thought, to tell you the truth. I never did, though. I never had to. That's what is funny.

I hallucinate. Did I mention that? That probably should have come first. But what are the metaphysics of psychosis, before even that? I'll visit this now. I am supposed to know about this, and this is the truth, whatever that also means… but I find myself less and less certain about its basic definition when it comes to other people, which, logically, would also indicate that I am at least certain about it to a small degree when it comes to me—but I am not. The term is meant to denote the event, or the process, of a consciousness finding itself disconnected and alienated from the world—from others' worlds, from the coalescent of worlds, as determined by other minds.

I see things. There we go—yes. I'll offer an anecdote. After work, last Friday, I was visiting a close friend. The day had ridden me analogous to how an obese toddler rides an old and tenacious dog. It had been particularly hot and sticky too. I had to make three house calls. There were too many words, too many vulgar expressions of too few base emotions. Strange insinuations, non-linear and nonsensical logical inferences, overpopulated a cornucopia of thoughts that lacked syntax. It all blended together into a mess, even in my immediate memory, that did little to accentuate whatever any individual third grader burped them. At any rate, I had wobbled up to her apartment as I usually did, the back of my head estranged by an inexplicable pressure most likely explained, at least to my consciousness, by the presence of a malignant fish weight.

She was chatting on the phone as she cooked, my friend, retelling some narrative about a recent experience at the movies. I was sitting on the couch. I was staring at the carpet. It was creamy and peppered. As fluid in my brain shifted to the right and the back of my head pulsated softly and tight, a dull and odious pain, familiar like a dithering aunt, and just as welcomed, returned to the cavity of my chest. The world shifted with the predilections of my awkward orientation.

"Wasn't the movie awesome?" my friend said from the kitchen. "No, no, I'm talking to Iosef. He's in the other room."

I waited a moment since it took me time to process the subtleties of her speech.

"Yeah," I said, full of exuberance.

But as I observed the homunculus operating the cognitive mechanics required for my response, my eyes stared vapidly ahead.

That was when the pepper specs became more prominent, dirtying the shag of the cream; they swelled, started to flicker and move. As I joined the change, the movement became quicker and abrasive. I cannot say that they were insects. They were not. Whatever came to life as I watched began to move like them though, and I remember that I hated myself for the cliché experience.

I closed my eyes. I took a breath. I took two deeper breaths and opened them. They were gone, but I knew they were there.

"Hey, let's go to the Bar and Grille this weekend," she said.

I didn't respond, partly because I wasn't sure if she was talking to me, partly because her sentence was just plainly unimportant.

"Hey, I said let's go to the Bar and Grille this weekend. Borges might be there."

I took another few moments.

"Sure," I said.

I remained in an intentional stupor, focused on my anti-thetical lack thereof. "The guy we met at the bar last weekend? Let's go. He's cute," I said.

I knew that if I wanted to, I could see them. All I had to do was search. All I had to do was become more open and simply conduct. Another world, so thinly askew, waited to bleed through the projector screen like ashen snow. My chest constricted. Silently, I made a decision. I heard her blather, but this time, I more so ignored her. She was disrupting my epiphany. I peered with my anti-focus.

The bugs didn't return. This time, a wind of black ash did. Entropy. I witnessed the forces of Entropy. And no one else could. No one else seemed to be as brilliant and prophetic as I, it seemed.

I also hear things too, and feel things. I hear the rumble of my thoughts, other peoples' thoughts, voices, perhaps my own, who can tell… The feeling thing is something that more so happens at night.

II

The office where I work out of is nestled between a domestic violence center and an allergy doctor. The building has a design reminiscent of a Christian community center from the early nineties. I remember that when I traveled there for the first time for my interview, I couldn't find it. Sitting right before a major crossway, my attention was too easily grasped by the choreography of cars and the strip mall and coffee shops beyond it. Until I really looked, it didn't exist. Well, I found it. Now I find it all the time.

I had to drag myself to work that morning. Sleep had become a cruel flirtation, rendering my wakefulness into a flat replica. It was a Monday and I had to attend office meetings on

Tuesdays. The only thing worse were Thursdays when I had to meet with coordinators for the county Department of Mental Health. I thought of all of this at once. I lost my appetite. I went straight to the coffee station.

"Good morning, Iosef," a co-worker said.

I smiled brightly after shoving my face in her direction. Jolie was her name, although I thought that it was funny that she even had a name considering that she was the typical middle-aged, overweight, and desperately curvy receptionist. I would say she was miserable and anxious, but this would be redundant and just as frivolous as her need for a name.

"Good morning," I said as I filled my mug. "How are you? How was your weekend?"

"It was alright," she said.

She did not expand; instead, she started fussing with a coffee filter.

"Cool," I said.

An expected silence passed between us. I used the time to casually take note of her nails, which were impeccably pink and decorated with rhinestones. As I sipped my coffee, I similarly observed the tightness of her paraprofessional clothing, which likened to the taut rind of an extraneously ripened plum. She continued to fuss. I saw her pupils shift to allow for a peripheral observation of my gaze. She also noticed that I noticed her observation of my observation. Neither of us made this exchange explicit. Before she met her pain tolerance for quietness, which would inevitably force another useless proposition upon which another futile conversation could be based, I walked away.

I set my briefcase beside my chair and settled my coffee mug on my desk. My eyes caught sight of the mess, of the uneven and scattered mounds of daily logs, messages, and reports with protected health information that required shredding. A young woman greeted me.

"You manage to catch up this weekend?" I asked.

"Of course not," she said, bubbly.

"Neither did I. I didn't work at all. I'm still four days behind."

She frowned.

"I'm sorry. I'm all negative," I said. "Let me try again. Good morning! What's on the agenda today?"

"I have a client coming in soon. Then I am going to work on catching up before going on visits. You?"

"Notes, notes, notes, I have to finish an assessment, and then I have to make a hospital visit," I said.

"Who?"

This question was nonsensical. She already knew.

"The Messiah."

"You're going by yourself? Why? You shouldn't do that."

Although she remained playful, her words were also scolding. She thought I was careless, or arrogant and ambitious—probably all of the above. I just shrugged.

"He's crazy. We just met about this last week. Don't go see him alone."

"I'll be alright," I said.

After rolling her eyes, she turned away to continue working.

Her name was Heidi Jones. Although we had worked together for about two years, we had only shared an office for approximately two months. I found this riveting. She was a clinical psychologist working on her Doctorate of Psychology. Her specialization was clinical psychology, of course. This is only a little beside the point. As a licensed clinical social worker, I was intensely curious of her work ethic and methodology. In all truth, I was also covetous. A practical doctorate would not suit my personality and ambitions, no—but nevertheless, regardless of my intention of attaining a Ph.D., or M.D., at that location in time and space, she was en route to becoming more decorated than I. And in the mental health field, such decorations provided force.

I had seen a plethora of her insecure case presentations, but until I shared an office with her, I had yet to really experience her interactions with clients. Now that I had, I was captivated by the dissonance of her presentation—she was attractive and suitably competent. However, her professional demeanor only accentuated the baselessness of her science. Ironically, it was the wobbly nature of her voice during her case presentations that purified her for my tastes. Such a tremor seemed to indicate honest deliberation. Her logic was oftentimes tenuous at best and pedestrian at worst, just like mine. Indubitably she suffered from the feedback loop of her conscience. And the grinding between her tongue and the pumice of her awareness produced the frailty in her voice.

She glimpsed at me from over her shoulder as she composed her reports. For once, I was not aware of this right away; it took me a few seconds. She must have caught me in my preponderant daze. My cheeks turned red. She smiled at me— and very genuinely. Diffidently, I mirrored her gesture.

I swung towards my computer monitor. My stomach sank. I looked at the clock, which informed me that it was already 9:30 am. I felt nauseous.

III

My anguish travelled the finest minutiae of my neurology—a charge, fervor, and zeal indescribable. Every muscle in my body contracted to force my body into tautness. My coat concealed it; nobody noticed, I think, but nevertheless, the flush made my brows gleam and this I could not so easily hide. I swiped it. For the umpteenth time, I mustered my strength.

But how quickly I was betrayed. My muse laughed at me. Within moments, I fell limp. A child homunculus somewhere peripheral to my awareness whimpered. I heard him. I snarled. I beat that little brat.

IV

Finally, I started to work.

My eyes locked onto the cursor wafting on the computer screen. I opened my Internet explorer. Checked my e-mail. Found nothing of interest there. Then persisted to locate my clinical software.

A pale gray screen manifested with a two-dimensional design. An obnoxious green logo contrasted with a dim steel background. I could not absorb the page further, although I saw it almost every day of my life. Either it was a problem with my visual memory, and this would not surprise me, or the image suffered from such poverty that no matter what, I could not etch it into the softness of my wax block.

I chose the 'create' button to write a new note. I scrolled down a registry of innumerable souls. After filling in some mundane details, I almost laughed sardonically; it was time to choose from an inane list of predetermined objectives and interventions. What was the objective related focus? 'Pro-social behavior.' Check. 'Medication compliance.' Check. Reflection over 'Triggers.' Check. Of course, none of these categories really packaged my experience. The interventions suffered just the same obtuseness. Explored client concerns for symptom management, prompted reflection for behavioral clarification, etc.

9:32 am. I buckled down after swallowing stomach acid. We had a scheme for writing the notes and I followed it: Problem, Intervention, Response, Plan.

Irene Garcia.

P: Client reported an intensification of depressive symptoms.

I: Thx (Therapist) performed a mental status exam. Thx explored client symptomology (onset, duration, frequency, intensity). Thx reflected content and emotion to clarify behavioral etiology. Thx offered validation, empathic support, and provided psychoeducation for universalization. Thx explored client's cognitive system further to continue the process of cognitive mapping. Thx gave client homework and contracted to follow up in a week.

R: The client appeared disheveled with a dysphoric effect. The client seemed oriented x4 (person, place, time, and situation) and demonstrated no gross impairments in cognition. The client presented without perceptual disturbance and without delusional content. The client claimed that she was free of methamphetamine abuse. In terms of her symptoms, the client reported that she has experienced moderate sadness and anxiety w/o panic attacks. She said she experienced an argument with her mother, which triggered memo-ries/automatic negative thoughts, exacerbating her symptoms. She isolated in response and ate less, stopped taking her medication. The client responded to empathic support and became more positive with engagement. The client recognized that she had a habit of ruminating on the thought, "Life is shit; I am worthless," every time she became stressed, and that this spawned a routine of isolation and irritable behavior. The client said she would list alternative interpretations of her argument and its consequences while also making note of her thought associations. Client contracted to remain medication compliant.

P: Thx to follow up and continue cognitive mapping.

I became disappointed. I realized that I had not 'investi-gated the client's perceptions and emotions associated with her discontinuation of medication.' What beliefs did she hold about her medication? Was she lying? Had she not been taking it for quite some time? How about the methamphetamine—I did not push there, although she potentially possessed all the signifiers of withdrawal…and why even focus on the medication?

"Hey, guys," a young man said, walking in.

I cringed. I peered down at my computer's clock. 9:43 am. My fingers found my keyboard in a flurry.

"Morning," I said distractedly, on purpose.

"Hey, Paul," Heidi said. "What's up? You'll never guess what happened to me this weekend."

"What? Did you check out Ferdinand's?"

"No, but I went to the other place with Jon."

"Where?"

"The Sycophant."

"Oh," he said with coyness. "You should have taken me."

"Maybe next time," she said. "Jon will be working anyway."

I tuned them out.

9:43 am.

Before navigating back to the main screen to create a new note, I glanced up at Paul. His hair was meticulously styled. Ruggedly placed dirty blonde waves parted to the right. To me, it looked too yuppie hipster hideous. Paul was a knock-off model, nevertheless. He was beautiful in the way that a copy of a piece of art retains the attractiveness of the original, but with unintended flaws of generational mutation.

I didn't realize that I kept staring and smiling again. "Yeah, I have to go there," I said, trying to play it off.

There was silence.

Paul stared.

Heidi laughed.

"We're talking about the rumor that they might want to hire someone as a lead therapist here, now," he said.

"Oh," I said.

I clicked another soul from the list. Her name was Lenore. I chose the objectives of reality testing and medication compliance, in addition to pro-social behavior and the completion of tasks. I slowly scrolled down and started checking a multitude of boxes for the interventions.

"Don't even try. He's not listening again," I heard Heidi say.

"I'm listening."

No, I wasn't. 9:55 am.

P: Client reported the presence of anxiety and depression symptoms.

"Dude, you need to relax," Paul said. "You're never going to catch up. We're all behind."

"Yeah, I have like nine days of notes to catch up on—and that's not even counting assessments," Heidi said.

I: Thx conducted mental status exam. Thx explored symptomology. Thx reflected content and emotion for behavioral clarification…

I stopped typing for a moment. My hands were still on the keyboard. "You know how this place goes. At any moment, we're going to be meeting. I need to get this done so I can go do visits and finish an assessment myself."

For the final 'R' and 'P' of this note, I quickly copy and pasted from another file. I glanced at the time. 9:57 am.

"What's your guys' percentages, anyway?" I said.

I didn't wait for an answer. Heidi said something. I didn't catch it. Peering over, I saw her eyes roll. Paul was gone. I went back to the main screen. Clicked the create button. Napoleon Gigante. A mercurial and cursory malaise chose the usual objectives and interventions that predetermined my next PIRP.

10:01 am.

We did not have a meeting that day. I was fortunate. My mind felt foggy. Instead of staying still, my thoughts played hide and seek with me—one moment, they would whisper to me in a speed nearly unintelligible and in the next, they would simply disappear into the stickiness. In these moments, I would stare vapidly. The funny thing is, though, no one seemed to notice. This told me that my colleagues were pitiful clinicians. 'Pitiful clinicians'… that phrase seemed redundant. There was no other genus. 10:30 am.

With a deep breath, I feverishly worked to complete the remaining six or seven notes requisite to justify the necessary percentage of billing for the previous day of labor.

V

Although I had an appointment at 11:00 am, I could not leave. Another social worker contacted me because his agency needed a letter. Our shared client, Lenore, whom I had just written about, required proof that she had been participating in individual therapy and/or substance abuse treatment for court. I found it hilarious that the and/or was included in the social worker's request. He was a child protective services worker, by the by. Apparently, he did not know what kind of services I provided. I agreed to do it. Then I took two steps and forgot.

10:46 am.

As I was walking out, I remembered, and most likely because of the phone call, that I had to place an important call myself. I quietly returned to my office, made sure no one else was present and picked up the phone.

Mr. Gigante had found himself in a psychiatric hospital, Valley Presbyterian, under very concerning circumstances regarding our agency and myself, and his attending psychiatrist had left me not one but two messages, which was why I was going to visit him. Apparently, he wanted to release him, but I wanted him to stay. During my visit, I was hoping to make my case. At any rate, I could only guess that my client had marijuana or methamphetamine in his system. When a client is 5150'ed by a qualified professional, which means they are detained against their will for either being a threat to themselves or another human being, or for being gravely impaired by their clinical disposition, they are placed on a 72 hour hold in the psychiatric ward of a hospital or urgent care so that he or she can stabilize. But when drugs are present they are often released early.

I reached a nurse.

"Hello, this is Iosef Guerrero. I am an FSP therapist calling from Recovery Clinics, and I received a call from one Dr. Garagousian. I was hoping to speak with him in regards to a client of mine, Napoleon Gigante. He was placed on 5150 this past Friday."

"Oh, yes. He was released this morning."

"He was released already?"

"Yes. This morning around 9:00 am. Hold on. Let me get you Dr. Garagousian."

She sounded abrasive. I couldn't help but wonder if she found me incompetent.

"Hello, this is Dr. Garagousian."

"Hi, nice to speak with you, this is Iosef Guerrero. I'm calling in regards to Napoleon Gigante. I'm his FSP therapist."

"Ah." He sounded dry.

I paused. Something wasn't right. He sounded too disdainful.

"Full Service Partnership. It's a type of program that provides individual and group therapeutic services intensively, while also offering case management and psychiatrist services. We do housing assistance for client stabilization. I'm calling from Recovery Clinics."

"I know what it is. Who is his psychiatrist?"

"Dr. Weisman," I said, more to the point.

"Well, Mr. Gigante didn't really have psychotic features. He denied audio and visual hallucinations, demonstrated only slight disorganization in behavior and speech, seemed minimally tangential, spoke without loose associations and altogether seemed oriented with little to no impairments in cognitive process or content. What are his medications?"

"Let me fetch his file."

After putting him on hold, it took me a minute or so to locate it. The files were disorganized. They were always disorganized. I rushed back to report my findings.

"Hello? Sorry about that. I'm familiar with his medications but I wanted to be sure. He is taking 15 milligrams of Zyprexa and 40 milligrams of Fluoxetine."

"What is his diagnosis?"

"When he first arrived at our agency," I said, pausing to clear my throat, "I diagnosed him with Psychotic Disorder, NOS. He reported audio hallucinations... hypnagogic visual phenomena, which I guess qualify as visual hallucinations... and, oh yes, yeah," I paused, "he demonstrated delusions of grandiosity and persecution with religious motifs. He displayed no negative markers or impairments of course and reported subjective experiences of depression and cognitive impairment, but without any exemplification in signs or behavior."

My voice sounded pressured. I couldn't breathe. I continued.

"Upon further inspection, Dr. Weisman and I made note of affective components, more notably, manic features triggered by substance abuse and other external stressors. As of now, his modified diagnosis is Schizoaffective Disorder, bipolar type..."

"The client claimed that he did not threaten to kill anyone."

"Well," I paused to steal a few deep breaths as inaudibly as I could. "Well...the client was here at the agency for his psychiatric appointment…however, he was not compliant with his medication regimen and forwardly psychotic."

I didn't know what I was saying.

"He presented without an inkling of grounding, or.., reality testing, and… well, put more succinctly, I'm sorry…oh, here we go." Haphazardly, I found the progress note that detailed this encounter. "The client demonstrated grave impairment due to his psychotic processes, which included a presentation of flight of ideas. He did not meet all criteria because he is currently living with his mother who helps provide for him. However, during a session with the client, where the psychiatrist was present, the client disclosed his intent to attempt harm upon myself and another undisclosed staff member."

"Alright," he said.

"You see," I laughed, "the client disclosed an entire delusional system that incorporated this agency. He ascribed to us a role of social control for some unseen, ominous elite class of individuals. He demanded that we cease our thought insertion and control and that we reimburse him for the damages incurred to him. I was actually hoping that you could hold him for a conservation process."

There was silence on the phone. "Hello?"

"That will be enough. The client was stabilized. We found traces of methamphetamine. He was discharged this morning. Goodbye."

I heard a click.

Had I sounded a fool? My tone—it must have conveyed my weakness, my lack of professionalism. The constriction became so painful.

In my chair, I sat, saying nothing, staring at the transparency of my own eyes.

11:05 am.

VI

I made my visits that day. But in all honesty, all I did was hold the space. I went home. Nobody was there with me. I already knew that. For approximately twenty-three minutes, I reinforced a very familiar narrative. Pathetic I was, a man without a mate, lacking in extra-laborious existence. I went to sleep—and by this proposition, what I mean to communicate is that I did not. All I did was pontificate in worship those sweet black sands.

CHAPTER TWO

I

The next morning I avoided the office. Instead of checking in like I was supposed to, I drove straight over to see my first client. All I had to do was call in: "I'm in the field." Unless there was an emergency, and who knew when that would be, my boss did not care. I imagined that he was just like me, except far more expired due to his place so much further down the line.

Antiquated buildings, ruinous yet elegant in their old-world cluttering, accented the bumpy road that delivered me to their dreariness. Mostly, the streets were abandoned where I was. Only a handful of rusty cars were asleep at the sidewalks. I smelled tamales, though, and that meant that some folks remained hidden within the grottoes. From all angles, I experienced the weight of their eyes.

As I meandered towards the dingy door of my client's apartment from my car, which I had parked two houses down on the opposite side of the street intentionally, I caught a glimpse of scurrying beyond the window beside her door. A knot of hesitation announced itself in my stomach. I glanced backward. My car was still there. Good. Had I locked it?

"Buenos dias, Iosef."

"Buenas."

Lenore chortled.

LE MARQUIS DE FOLIE

"Yah, yah, yah—I'm a twinky," I said.

"I need to teach you Spanish."

I looked back again, unsure.

"You write my letter?" she said.

"Of course."

"My social worker said he didn't get it."

"I sent it." I lied. "I'll fax it again."

"Ok, you can come in then."

Intuitively, I positioned myself on the part of her sofa that was closer to the door. Lenore bustled about nearby in the half-kitchen of her two bedroom apartment. She offered me a glass of water, which I denied as friendly as I could. So she started to prepare me coffee instead. The aroma put me somewhat at ease.

"So how are things going today?" I said.

"Ok, ok. I have to pick up my kids from school in the afternoon. So busy today. I still have to call and find out about my bills." She paused for a moment as she continued bustling. "This place is a mess. I'm so embarrassed."

Although it was far from pristine, her place actually struck me as tidy. Lenore lived with her two children in addition to her brother-in-law, although the latter, reportedly, was never there. Only a few sticky splotches marred the glass table, which otherwise wasn't dusty. I could see a few dark spots on the grayish carpet, but it did not seem too greasy. A billion trinkets and lackluster toys weathered from what seemed to be generations of childish torture cluttered her domicile, giving her miscellaneous decorations a strangling effect, but given her situation, this didn't strike me as inappropriate.

"Looks clean to me. You should see my place."

She waved her arm from the kitchen.

"How are you this morning? You have anything else you have to do? I don't want to be a bother," I said.

She sat the coffee pot in front of me after pouring me a cup with a mischievous gleam. She very well knew that I wouldn't touch it.

"Nope, just you and me."

I felt my cheeks warm.

"You're such a baby," she said.

The play in her accent was coquettish.

"Last time we met," I said, "we discussed your progress in regards to your treatment goals. You haven't used methamphetamine or cocaine in six months, which is a significant achievement, and you report that you are experiencing your spells of sadness and panic attacks three times a week—a drop off from a frequency of five times per week."

She continued to stare at me in a manner that struck me as simultaneously seductive and condescending.

"You're horrible." I gave her a pleading look. "Come on, focus."

"Your mom and dad must be very proud of you."

"Well." Again, I turned red. "Oh, well, thank you. But—"

"I don't know, Iosef. I guess I've gotten better. But I still feel the same."

There was a long silence.

"Can you tell me more?" I said.

"I've been feeling really sad and tired lately. I've always felt sad and tired. I *am* sad and tired."

"You don't feel like you've had any improvements in mood and energy? In past sessions, you've definitely struck me as more energetic."

She shrugged.

"How's your sleep?"

"It's alright."

"How many hours per night? And do you wake up?"

"Probably like six hours a night, and yes. I make up for it though when I wait to pick my kids up."

"When do you get to bed these days?"

"Depends. Sometimes at eleven, sometimes at one or three."

"Well, we've already covered the importance of maintaining a structured day for ADLs, and of the absolute pertinence—well, importance—of getting enough rest and going to bed and waking up around the same time. You'd be surprised at the shift in your energy and restfulness, and in your experience of predictability that can definitely enable you to better cope with anxiety and stress."

She had become dryly placid.

"You'd even be surprised at what it can do for the mood."

"I know."

"You have been taking your medication?"

"Yes."

"Any relapses?"

"No."

She looked away; so did I. Her shoulders slouched, long in want of her former coquettishness. After fingering my cup of coffee, I persisted in boycotting its contents. I forced myself to reestablish a friendly eye contact. With it, I fought with the effects of the boreal air. Her frigidness melted away.

"I'm sorry. You know what? I'm a terrible therapist."

"—What? No. No, I'm sorry, mijo. It's just my mood. You're very sweet, and you're trying to help me. I'm just negative, that's all."

"Let's slow down for a moment. I'm going to dissect what you just said as a good example of what I'm trying to get at. I have your attention?"

"Yes."

"My job is not to be sweet. Don't get me wrong…it's not to be an asshole, either. But I am not here to be nice and amicable. Similarly, I'm not here to play the role of surrogate nephew or son in a sympathetic manner to try and brighten your day. I'm here to be a resource for you to utilize so that you can troubleshoot and improve your life. Still with me?"

She nodded.

"Ok. That said...I'm a terrible therapist." I laughed to summon within her a chuckle. "I guess you haven't done the homework I assigned you?"

"No...no, I haven't." She pursed her lips. "I'm sorry."

"The idea behind it, as I explained before, is that by exploring the thoughts that pop into your head whenever you feel sad and tired, or before this, and your subsequent actions, however, small they might be, we can become more conscious and aware of your routines so that we can institute changes. However, I'm getting the message that you're just not feeling it."

"I want to, I do, trust me—I just don't have the motivation. I tell myself every morning after I drop the kids off that I'm going to do it, but then I get home and feel so tired. And then I get frustrated and just lay down to close my eyes."

"Precisely. And my job isn't to keep hitting you over the head with something that you have not been able—well, with something that isn't really appropriate for what you're experiencing."

I stopped.

"Let's do this. Think about your treatment goals—"

"I don't want to feel this way. I want to sleep less. I want to be a better mother for my kids. And I want to do something. I want to work—but how can I? I need my social security. If I work, I'll lose it, and then what? And what sort of job will hire *me* that will pay me more and that will be worth it?"

This was not the first time I had heard those words. My oxygen grew heavy and settled on the ocean floor of my abdomen. I willed no sigh. I choked on my undigested juices.

"We'll start there again next time. I want you to think about what is possible for you *right now*. What you think the first step can be. Ok? And we'll draw a new map from there."

"Ok."

"Call me if you need anything."

"Ok. Bye, Iosef. Thank you for coming. I don't know what I'd do without you."

As I walked outside, I made sure to investigate the safety of my car. After this, I signaled goodbye to her with a cordial wave.

II

When I arrived, the office appeared desolate. As I hurried through the back entrance to the clinic, I caught a glimpse of a meeting through the crack of the conference room door. The corpulent cheeks of Mr. Giuseppe suffered from the creases of his pompous, impassioned expression. We locked eyes for but one second; he didn't motion me in. He appeared to be leveling down his bi-monthly schooling. I had the sinking suspicion that my good name fell victim to the fiery winds of his irascible didacticism.

I fled into my office. I didn't have time for that. Eight progress notes, an assessment, a coordinated client care plan, one letter, three flex fund requests, and four phone calls commanded my existence with a force almost equal to the beholding, veiny spheres of my supervisor.

For but a moment, I rested my head on my desk. I was not tired. No, I was not tired. That was the lie that I told myself.

Someone lunged upon my shoulders.

"Hey, Guerrero," Paul said. "Whoa, calm down. Jumpy are we?"

He sounded too cheery.

"Hey, I didn't miss our meeting, did I?" I said.

"No, no—don't worry. That was an ad hoc meeting to discuss the usual lag in billing and notes. DMH might be auditing our files, too, so we have to start dedicating one day a week to actually fixing our files."

His brow furrowed. He must have noticed my frustration.

"Relax. You're alright. Once again, you need to calm down."

"How am I supposed to calm down when I am so behind, and when so many of my clients are not making any progress?"

I couldn't tell if his affectation conveyed sympathy, empathy, or some breed of contempt. He didn't say anything; he merely stood there, his hands on his waist.

"Of course *you're* not worried," I said. "You're all caught up, and—"

"And?"

You always pander to Mr. Giuseppe anyway, I thought.

I waved him off. "Let me do my notes."

"Alright. Lunch later?"

"Sure."

I left early.

III

My final visit of the day was to the hovel of Napoleon Gigante. He lived deep in squalid and foreign lands. Of course, I chose the time of my foray intentionally. If I went on my expedition too late into the afternoon or evening, the streets would be rife with wanton juvenile propensities and their opposition, a police force almost colonial in disposition. I managed to avoid them, having driven over in a rush at approximately 1:00 pm. I warranted strange stares from passing police cruisers as per the usual. However, I was accustomed to that—and in all honestly, profoundly thankful for their Cossack sensibilities.

Lenore's neighborhood was poor and dangerous, yes—but Napoleon's struck the senses as eerie and ominous. I did not feel like I even remained in the United States. Instead, I felt like I had irreverently entered the Gaza strip.

After parking, I quickstepped to the Gigante residence— and by that, I signify a cave within the caverns of the projects. The courtyard was empty. Nevertheless, the presence of an invisible and nefarious surveillance gave my gait a fastidious swagger. Every time I came here, I felt like a foreign emissary draped in velvet robes embroidered in gold.

"Hello? Ms. Gigante?"

I knocked loudly.

"Napoleon?"

I waited. No answer.

I had to battle the onset hyperventilation.

"Hello, it's Iosef—Napoleon's *therapista*."

One minute fulfilled the dictates of my personal con-science. I had fulfilled due diligence. Before long, I was home.

IV

Have you ever felt *terribly* alive? Perhaps in asking this question, I am already squandering any hopes of communica-tion. Don't miscomprehend; I am a dead man. But I am also a live one. Ha —I am so *tuft* with fervor. What does that even mean, tuft? See. That was the wrong word. I am electrified— mortified—electrocuted; I am burning, buzzing, thrilling, bouncing—but compacted, constrained, oppressed, predetermined, controlled—and controlling. What other words whirl and unfurl. Oh, really, it is all very dreadful, this being. Insurmountable, even—so I must surmount other things, objects, beings, subjectivities. I am even misdirecting you right now—but now that I have told you this, is this not misdirecting in itself in quite the duplicitous manner? Paucity, this mind—I am conversing with my mind.

V

I paced back forth in my room, the telephone still in my hand.

"Why do you stay at that job?" Lucia said. "You're always complaining about it. Quit."

"Uh huh," I said. "And what am I supposed to do then?"

"Is it worth your life?"

"Nothing is going to happen."

"Uh huh," she said.

I was lost, gawking at my computer screen.

"We take precautions. I am trained to take precautions. Trust me, I'll be fine," I said.

"Then why did you call me?"

"To chat."

Now, I stared at the floor. She said something unimportant. My eyes felt gashed. I couldn't find the black in the breeze. Hurriedly, I sat down but then quickly got up again. I harassed the keyboard, fiddling about a purchase screen. She said more unimportant things.

"Yes, yes, Borges is too cute," I said.

I clicked 'buy.'

"Yeah. Let's go this weekend. Totally," I said. "He might not be there, but we'll see. If he is, I'll make sure to talk to him."

Arising, I walked over to my dresser, feeling like I had left something; no, no, I forgot nothing. I hurried back.

"Ok, love you. I'll see you this weekend," she said.

Where was the black?

"Bye. Love you," I said.

My credit card, that was what I forgot—it was still in my wallet, which was usually on the dresser. After speeding over to retrieve it, I realized that it wasn't there. Instead, my wallet was behind a recent book of scant interest, some insignificant philosophical work by Wittgenstein, which was shoved back, hidden and forgotten amidst the clutter on my floor.

Something unsettled me, but doubt only ruled the spineless. There came a time when every woman or man had to resolutely rebel and strike only with vehemence and the solipsistic ethicality of the bitter slave, revolt in contradistinction to their ethereal bindings, confabulate and accept their being, and charge forth without any regard for that old Majesty; in short, I had to be a Duke, not a Bon-Bon. At that moment, I put down my black dog. I surrendered. I was terribly alive.

My friend, her words, those slippery meanings, her fraudulent soothsay: how could she speak with such subterranean whispers? I should quit? I should be careful? She *loved* me?

I entered my pseudonym. The world would know my thoughts. They would never recognize me or comprehend, this was likely. However, they would be touched; they would be unable to forget. For once the imagination is molested, countless creatures are engendered in its inextinguishable fertility.

And with encephalitic focus, my prolegomena was born:

Allô!

Welcome to my confessional. I work as a mental health therapist. What does this mean? *Excusez-moi de vous déranger,* but it means that I, too, am mentally ill. I am not lying. More specifically, though, it means that I harbor a universe of secrets, which are both my own and of others. Since this is my confessional, however, and since I am bound by honor to respect the law of confidentiality, this place will only concern my own—and yours—if you wish.

Have you ever been curious about what your therapist was really thinking and experiencing while talking with you? Do you have questions concerning mental health? Are you a therapist, as well, and are seeking anonymous advice—or rather, a place to also think and confess?

Do you wish to articulate your imagination, your *grain de fantaisie*? Or, perhaps, you wish to merely voyeur?

Then this clinic is for you.

Take a walk around. If for anything, do it for the psycho-education. We'll speak behind the curtains.

Adieu!

Le Marquis de Folie

VI

An hour past midnight, I managed to sleep—but in my dreams, a malaise did stalk me. Someone, anyone, might indeed discover my page—oh threatened the thought—I had a conversation about this, with myself, I vaguely remember. I woke up, or more like I stirred to a more full and drowsy consciousness, from the rude suffocation of postnasal mucus. After taking a few strained and anxious breaths, I flew to my computer and tore down my site.

CHAPTER THREE

I

That weekend, I met Lucia at the Bar and Grille. Borges was there. Never had I seen my dear companion so overcome. Borges was another Paul, this rapscallion—but perhaps a little more renowned in his libertine aplomb. When I laid my eyes upon him, I had the faintest dawning, the creepiest little sensation, that the man kept locked within him a soul most prodigious. And of course, this was evidenced by the unquestionable debonair with which he had been sipping at his whiskey sour. Things were going to change soon, so this night was memorable. In fact, I sort of remembered it as the prolegomena to the fall, and thus it will serve as such.

I bumped my friend forward. Her bony shoulder obstructed, without a doubt, Borges' smug linear assumptions concerning the profligate tidings of his night. The clink of the shoddy whiskey glass against his tooth made my friend's eyes light up in horror.

"Ah!" he said.

"Oh my god, I'm so sorry," Lucia said.

I saw her cursing at me silently.

"Oh, shit. Hey-," I said.

Borges looked entirely too concerned with the integrity of his incisor. His friends glared at us for him.

"That was my fault. I accidentally caused all that." I laughed foolishly and apologetically. "Borges, right?"

He recovered quickly. "Yeah."

With one last rub to his tooth, which appeared to have survived the collision, he seemed much more certain of his place in the world again and smiled—at first hesitantly, but then with the full luster of his charm with which my friend had become helplessly obsessed. His gestured for his friends to continue towards the bar.

"...Lucia, right?" he said.

"I see you're still in the same metro bullshit," she said.

"Again with that? I only paid forty dollars for this sweater."

She wiped some droplets of whiskey off its felt. "What a shame."

Her figure cocked, victorious in its facetiousness. When she was flirtatious, she was mean. Once his friends returned with drinks, everyone finally relaxed—and even I did after a few sours of my own, which I went for myself as an excuse to get away. Borges and her exchanged numbers, eventually. And although this event in itself did not indicate my dear friend's victory, the fact that the bar seemed to become quiet and still for him did. For it is difficult to concentrate, I am sure, for any man, and especially a Borges, when inculcated, and just by mere presence, into the nearby mischief of kittens.

For the rest of the weekend, all I heard about was this Borges. We spent that Saturday together too, Lucia and I; however, she was mostly engrossed by the tickles of her phone. Scarcely could I hold her attention. Between the digital pigeons from Borges and her personal vacations into lewd reveries, there existed only scraps of her affections. This didn't necessarily bother me and neither did the fact that I had not met a girl. I required time to reflect and to write. Besides, have you not ever provided happiness? Eudemonia, for those of us who are only extrinsically of the Good, can arguably be experienced solely through the graces of such refractions. Nevertheless, it was indeed an introduction to an end.

II

How is it possible to know when a problem is spiritual; what knowledge provides us with this direction? —What species of evidence forms the 'elements' of this knowledge?

I was lost. That didn't stop these questions from haunting me.

III

We started late. Our Tuesday meeting was scheduled for 9:30 am. I arrived on time. I put everything aside. As the moments escaped, and my anxiety peaked its head to mourn the sheer loss of time, and as I ruminated over the usual loop of torture in regards to my tasks, I held hands with all the positive spirits I could in order to expurgate my obsession.

"Alright," Mr. Giuseppe said. "First, I'd like to say that everyone has been doing a great job. We are doing alright. Are we doing perfectly? Of course not, but we are making things happen. I am proud of each and every one of you. I'm glad to say that we're one of the best teams out there."

In tone, our supervisor's applauding of us seemed perfunctory and routine. Everyone looked fidgety and bored. However, I couldn't help but to notice more interest than usual. Mr. Giuseppe hardly ever called meetings with the entire staff. Something was different.

"We have three things on the agenda today," he said. "Productivity, case presentations, and some great news. We already discussed productivity last week, so I'll just update that point. Guerrero, 55 percent—shame on you."

Instead of continuing, he stole a long moment to purvey his dissatisfaction, making awkward eye contact with me first, and then with the rest of the room, in a manner that was playful but bullying. My cheeks blanched to clear the way for the blood. Paul and Heidi chuckled. Quickly, I tried to get in on the joke but this did not stem the symphony of laughter at my expense.

"Ok, ok—Paul, 79 percent. I don't know what you're doing, but keep it up. Heidi, 60 percent—not bad. Nina, you have 57 percent. Marian—and you," he shuffled through his papers, perhaps for more effect again. "You have 35 percent."

"That's ludicrous. That can't be right. All my notes and daily logs are in," she said.

"I know that I'm not caught up. It's been a crazy week," I said, trying to defuse things, "but like I always say, those numbers aren't exactly reflective of my labors. I do my own math. I am never below 70 percent. I'm sure it's the same situation with you, Marian."

"Ok, ok, ok," Giuseppe said. "We get it, we know. The percentages are off. They only account for what has been billed, not what has been done. But it's relative, yes? Paul has, what, 80 percent? That means he's probably really in the 90's."

Paul looked away.

"We're almost meeting our goals. Remember, DMH requires that we account for 65 percent of our day with direct services in the field. We're doing good, but we all need to pull our own weight. That's the bottom line. So I'm not going to dwell on this point. I trust each and every one of you to do what it takes. Let's move on to case presentations."

He nodded to Paul. "Go ahead."

"Oh. Ohm. Yeah." Paul cleared his throat. "Ok. I'll start with William DeWitt. Some of us are already familiar with him. He was admitted to the program about two weeks ago. His assessment and CCCP are complete."

He took a deep breath before continuing. "This man is crazy."

Everyone laughed.

"He is a 35-year-old African-American male. He presented appropriately dressed for the weather, but I think that might be coincidental. Anyway, he is disheveled, doesn't attend to his ADLs, and presents with a blunted affect."

I leaned forward and extended a hand.

"Paul, could you clarify the terminology since we are in a general meeting?"

"Oh, sorry, that's clinical language. ADLs basically mean the required activities of daily living, like hygiene, eating, drinking, and so forth. When I say he has a blunted affectation, it means that he has an inability to convey any emotion whatsoever. The CCCP is just our clinical plan for the county." He nodded to me. "Good note. Anyway. He is a very impaired individual. He did not seem oriented to time or situation, and it wasn't clear whether he had a lucid comprehension of himself. He was referred to us from St. Dymphna IMD and carries a diagnosis of Schizophrenia, disorganized type. He was a poor historian due to decreased prosody and impaired memory, remote and recent. He claimed his presenting problem was that he 'couldn't talk to people,' although according to his paperwork, he was institutionalized for being gravely disabled and petty theft. He reported no symptomatology. But I noticed the following—loose associations in his thought process and communication in addition to, it goes without saying, tangential and circumstantial dysfunction. At moments, he mumbled incoherently, indicating word salad. He also seemed to speak with neologisms. I witnessed the client reacting to internal and external stimuli as well, which would seem to be evidential of auditory and visual hallucinations. I did notice paranoia, but William did not verbalize his experience of it. And of course,

33

the client presented with disorganized behavior. According to—"

"Could you inform us about just what you noticed that would make you think he was disorganized and paranoid?" I said.

"What do you mean?"

"Well," I said, "it isn't uncommon for any individual to display phenomena that could be interpreted as disorganized for other reasons. For instance, if someone is shy for whatever behavioral cause, they might speak less. If they have been institutionalized, they might be guarded, which could present like paranoia. You get the point."

"Oh." He gave me a look. "I see where you're going." He laughed. "Ok, Iosef. To exemplify…" He paused, holding his nose up ever so slightly to accentuate his mocking. "…The client would experience punctuations of near-catatonic decompensation following brief interfaces with shiftless, directionless pacing. His stare would be empty, and he would experience obvious thought stopping."

"But you are describing subjective states of mind. You have no access to this client's inner world. How can you be so certain of these words you are using to describe his signs and behavior?" I said.

"You raise interesting questions," Mr. Giuseppe said. He was barely suppressing his sardonic expression. "We'll talk about them in supervision."

"We are here to discuss these cases as a team," I said. "The words we use have influence. What if this William is not as psychotic as we think but we do not consider this? Our collective dialogue determines the direction of his treatment. We need to discuss and consider different interpretations."

"He has a point," Marian said.

Mr. Giuseppe inhaled deeply. Paul did the same, but his breathing was quicker. I was surprised to see that he looked more remorseful and nervous than chided.

"Alright Mr. Smart Guy," Mr. Giuseppe said. "With your extensive clinical knowledge, present to us the different possible interpretations then."

"Well, I can't. I haven't seen this client. I would need to know more details about his history and disposition."

"Oh! Interesting. You mean you would need to know more about the client before speaking with any education on the matter?" He gestured to Paul and quite frivolously. "Go ahead."

"Sorry for interrupting," I said.

Paul continued. His tone was almost apologetic at first, and for my regard. I couldn't help but to seethe. He quoted from the IMD's psychiatric and medical reports at length although he had absolutely no access to their esoteric meanings. People fawned with every medical utterance, at every grotesque syllable. In all, I believe he went on for ten minutes about some multidimensional treatment approach to strike at the numerous facets of this man's Axis I diagnosis, although, and I quote, "research presently indicates that mental illnesses are all expressions of Axis III dysfunction." The client would be drug tested to ensure the absence of substance abuse, be linked with psychiatric services for psychotropic medicinal intervention, and engaged in individual and group therapy for behavioral modification and the acquisition of coping skills insofar as the client demonstrated the developmental and 'cognitive-behavioral-affective' prerequisites. Paul eruditely referenced the recovery model. There was almost applause. Oh, the marvel that was his articulate clinical wizardry.

In short, he advocated the very same treatment plan that we so dutifully midwifed for every other client at our agency—

and each time with the airs of singularity, with all the fanciful display of masterly artisanship.

I stayed quiet—but I exaggerate not, inside, a metaphysical consumption vitiated my composition.

In time, I found out why Paul went on for so long—I discovered the reason for his inspired tomfoolery. After Heidi gave an astute and meticulously organized case presentation, superior in form, yet necessarily handicapped in profundity, and after I also had to give one of my own—an empty update on the state of Napoleon Gigante that was summarily ignored—Mr. Giuseppe impishly celebrated his third order of business.

"Paul is now the lead therapist for FSP and FCCS," he said. "He has demonstrated his competency and leadership. Everyone here was qualified and would have been great for the position...But we were forced to choose a candidate based on prior experience and seniority at the company. Nonetheless, I am absolutely certain that he will make an excellent clinical supervisor."

The conference room imploded in the following vacuum, which of course naturally preceded a conflagration of congratulations from all directions and corners of the building.

Paul turned red. So did I. I congratulated him, of course, and jubilantly. And you know what, I truly meant it.

I was authentically happy for him. But at the same moment I also felt hate. This Tuesday defined me. It was my workaday, plodding fall. My reaction was also underwhelming and this, quite assuredly, was yet another symptom of my disease.

IV

"You are going to die, Guerrero."

Everyone was gone. I read the threat on Instagram while sitting in my office. Napoleon had also left me three separate voicemails wherein he made the vow to rape my children. These children of mine, existing in his universe although not in mine, required purification through the distilling potency of his messianic phallus. Such propositions, very much familiar to me, unsurprisingly decorated the otherwise bland aesthetic of his social networking profile. Thank the Lord—and of course, by the Lord I meant him—that such nefarious prose found its heart in all the banality of such a vulgar medium. The absurdity of it all inspired within me a chuckle. In the twenty-first century, it seemed, God condemned heathens, such as myself, not through the humdrum of the most insipid of biblical maladies, but rather via the relentless pestilence of a different kind: those of that despicable *genus*, 'status update.'

In a click, I found his profile photo. In it, he posed in a manner reminiscent of a conquistador—at least, that was how it appeared to me. He had greased his dark brown hair forward and over his face. Such a style actually fit him, however; he was dark skinned but paler than he should have been, and wide-eyed. And I had to admit, he struck me as quite photogenic—right there, in that photo, I witnessed all of his tragic predilection for romantic suffering. For a second, I was almost covetous.

I decided to read one of his nonsensical ramblings. For some reason unknown to me I performed it aloud. I suppose I was curious to see what it felt like to experience his thoughts as if they were mine.

"I am depressed and anxious. I can't say that I'm saying ti right. But I have reached the highest level of consciousness I am Napoleon born again on earth, and I have been witness to the thousansth degree of absolute clarity in relation to all the world gods [fake gods] who seek to control [insert, deocrify, submiss] my eternal blessings, for I have risen and been born [recreated, rejuvenated, remaximized] in order to bring the great fathoming of our Savior [myself, Napoleon reborn,

Gigante Christ Lucifer x9***]. All will be raped and purified by my dark light. Go now and scribble my name on all walls and signs and you will be saved for the Fathoming [great fathoming, not lesser fathoming -3x1**]. All of my enemies [allies] seek out the traitor brander oppressor Iosef Guerrero. He and everyone at Recovery Clinics must beg for emrcy as they are tortured and raped with all the acidic [10x's stronger acidic than anything known to mere mortals] phantasmal power only this will be your saving degree of earnestness in the eys of the Savior [Napoleon x2* Lucifrist Gigante Yaweh]."

There were pages upon pages of this. Litanies of comments in reference to one another scanned down the page of each photo without any visible end. No matter how far down I scrolled and clicked, the arabesques of his psychotic effluvium continued. This was his universe; here, his cosmology reigned. Quickly I fled the realm of my Dark Savior. I closed the browser. I took a breath.

After I had finished my reports, and in-office sessions for the day, I called him back. In all honesty, I was nervous. He didn't answer. My prayers were granted.

Of course, he didn't answer. Why would he? Why would the Savior lower himself to answer *my* call?

Thirty minutes passed. I was ready to leave, and there you have it, the Dark Savior commanded my work phone.

I hit ignore.

CHAPTER FOUR

I

Shallow, my breaths were shallow due to the density of my bedroom air. For how long had I been swallowing this smut? By then, it wasn't 'air' at all—it was the poison expelled from my lungs, 'the chickens returning home to roost.' The fact that this paraphrase manifested within my head to signify my existence only exacerbated my illness. Had I willed such a thought? My thoughts suffered from such banality.

I gazed blankly at the back of my eyes as I suffocated. Very briefly I found enough focus to catch the time on my alarm clock. 12:07 am.

What was I still doing awake? I scolded my own person, whatever that means. How was I to understand what was happening to me? Did any *valid* and *reliable* explanation exist? With this thought, my paresthesia became evident to me. My phalanges, my extremities felt tingly and strange, like they were foreign and only now checking into customs. This was a neurological function and evidence of a pervasive underlying problem of this nature. "Lord, have mercy upon me," I thought. No, he wanted me raped.

I sat in silence to force a new equilibrium. I don't know how many times I had done this. What did I mean to do? I was a trained psychotherapist. I knew grounding techniques. Allegedly, I was a master of consciousness, of recreation, of the process of 'actualization' wherein the wretched soul sublets their mechanically delimited negativity during a process of midwifery.

Tranquility. I sensed that it was near. I closed my eyes to snuggle myself into an imagined serenity of some big bubble. In and out, I respired. As I did so, I allowed my fingers to massage my bed sheets upon which I laid. Without any conscious willing, I found that my massages quickly became caresses of a seductive sort, and a bestial desire awakened as I attempted to rest.

My sympathetic system remained activated, I inferred— which means that I was not truly at rest; however, at least I had inverted my ill-temper.

How did I know?

And what did grounding even mean? If my problem, etiologically, was neurological, then what did it matter that I 'grounded' myself? —at least in the long-term. Grounding, if it meant settling in this manner, equated only to a learned stoic resilience. And what were the metaphysics of this grounding? My profession often employed this technique contra anxiety and negative ruminations. When a human being experiences dysentery in their nerves, the loose running of their mind often correlates, it alleges. In this situation, grounding is mediated form of reality testing. Such foolery, however—never had I heard any colleague of mine consider the problem of such a proposition. For to posit that 'grounding,' herein meant also as a form of 'reality' testing, slows the mind enough to reunited it with 'reality,' with the sensual world, is to cling to the epistemic dogma that our cognitions, when healthy, correspond 'appropriately'—and this is a euphemism for truthfully—to an object.

What if by grounding myself I was only corroborating my chains?

Then I should not ground myself, for to do so would be to strengthen the fortitude of my shackles.

When I opened my eyes, I did so without focus—that is to say, I did so with my *anti-focus*. And I was greeted by the dizzying flurry of colorful static in the darkness of my bedroom and as I tried to (not)look, very quickly did this estranged blur morph into the familiarity of my black snow. For a good ten minutes, I was its spectator, mesmerized. They appeared to me as the quark meteorites of a new cosmic dawning, cascading across the plastered skies of my bedroom cage.

CHAPTER FIVE

I

Approximately a month and a half had passed since that Tuesday.

Altogether, my disposition had improved. Things weren't so fragmented for me, any longer. I had made peace with myself. I didn't get the promotion, but I had never fathomed that I would get it anyway. And I admired Paul. He was a good man. My sleep had also been much better, too. While before I was lucky to get four or five hours a night, now I could accomplish at least seven. As a result, my mood was more euthymic and I wasn't experiencing all the strange thoughts and visuals that had tormented me for so long. No longer did I have night terrors. Additionally, my memory, my awareness didn't feel as choppy or foreign. Funny, how episodic things could be. In fact, I want to apologize to you for my tone, and for the sporadic, jarring, and even artificial flow of my narrative thus far. Sometimes, I cannot help it. I could have made it seamless. I could have made the narrative mostly linear and continuous. However, it would not have been true. So, in a way, it had to be. One must suffer to understand, although some things are best left omitted since they are just too painful. But you're here now and it should get better. I promise.

Anyway, I was feeling more social, finally. I had even gone on a date, although I never called the girl back. Well, it was sort of a date. Borges and Lucia had continued to talk and I had joined them on a double.

He wasn't a terrible person, Borges. He was an actor, which was exciting for Lucia. With his looks, his chosen vocation did not surprise me—he made quite the ideal type. What I really liked about him, though, was his depth of knowledge in relation to character. Psychotherapists and actors hold much in mutual esteem, I discovered. He was political, too, and often asked me about my writing. At any rate, Lucia adored him. As a student of history and an activist, she needed someone who could enjoy ideological banter.

"Iosef," Borges said, waving at me.

"Nice of you to show up," Lucia said. "Dude," she looked around carefully and lowered her voice to bar whispers, "there's a hot girl that's so cool. She would totally love you."

"Oh, ok," I said.

"You're such asshole. What was that face?"

"He just got here, leave the man alone," Borges said, wafting at her neck. "Watch out for the bar girl so we can order a drink. What's your drink tonight?"

"Sazerac," I said. "Well, let me get them."

"No way, I got it," he said.

A fine lord of douchebaggery passed by our table. A cheesy upturned mustache juxtaposed with his masculine shadow, all of which complimented his olive smoke jacket and extraneously gelled helmet. We crossed cursory glances and then I saw the maenad behind him. For a moment, I experienced a knot in my stomach. Then I felt awe. She was a parade, this woman. I could tell that she was also a succubus and I wanted her.

I couldn't wait to get out of the booth. "No, really. They're on me. You got drinks last time. I'll go to the bar. This could take forever."

Lucia sneered.

"What?" I said.

Borges kissed her on the side of her fuming head. He snuck me a mischievous and fraternal look.

"I'll take a Sazerac," he said.

"Cool. I'll be right back."

As I walked away, I could hear her scolding him. "Don't encourage him, you don't know him like I do. He needs a good girl."

I stayed away for quite some time due to the busyness of the bar. That was usually the case on a weekend. Such desperation—the way every soul thronged the counter reminded me of desiccated beasts at the mirage of a deluge. The workweek was their desert. Herein, at this miserable hole, awaited their rationed teases of a reverie. I did not rush as they did. I had my ulterior motives, which, I supposed, at a place such as this, weren't actually so ulterior.

Although I had lost sight of the maenad, one of the most beautiful women I had ever seen seemed midway through the capture of a thrall to my left. She appeared to be Armenian. Her mundane name was trivial, of course. I bestowed upon her a truer title known only to Plato's lords and daemons: Astghik. She smiled a lustful sun and adjusted her locks of obsidian perfection. I saw the eyes of the child before her. They locked upon her sultry, plush lips, which seemed to move with such a graceful finish that I additionally suspected the aid of magic. Quite the fool, this child turned his back to purchase her gin. I guess in this situation, the barkeep would be Anubis or something—my metaphor was not perfect. At any rate, I caught her sly exchange with what I assumed to be one of her Dionysian kindred. Something wicked laughed in her triumphant smirk. Mastication would continue, I surmised, and then she would move on to the next of the abundant and sanguine meek.

There was no shortage of these goddesses and gods. I spied a Xochiquetzal or two, or three—each of them readily adorned by at least a small audience of worship for the sacrifice. To the far east reigned a Rati. She giggled a lot. And with every strike of her banshee melody, her servants blushed with sangria for her tasting. Freyja and Cliodhna took turns sipping at the tall glass of a mere lad's whiskey. And of course, after some searching, I found an Aphrodite and a Venus, and a Bestet and a Qetesh. And the carcasses upon which they delightfully testified to God their maleficent and narcissistic luminance constituted a contemporary Golgotha of witty moths' broken wings bewitched.

I gawked in amazement. The men bored me. Fewer, those of the qualia of Pothos, but they were nevertheless plentiful enough to pre-eradicate my contestation. They preyed like lionesses on even the heroines. I hated them but, of course, and I loathe myself to say this, I also adored them, and I also thusly hated myself. And it was with this odiousness that I finally took my spot at the spigot.

"Two Sazeracs and an Old Fashioned," I said.

I failed to get the barkeep's attention. I said it again, practically yelling. He flinched, glared at me shortly, and nodded before letting the chaos of the demand recapture him. I leaned against the sticky wood of the bar to appreciate the dashes of the men and women holding down the siege. The barkeep looked to have a seizure as he shook a signature drink, perhaps my own.

Peripherally, I made subtle note that the maenad, the Qandisa, who had previously been following the illustrious lord of the mustache, stole the stool beside me. I had the distinct suspicion that she, at that very moment, welcomed my attention.

She glanced over. I flinched away.

The barkeep slammed my drinks down, almost making a splash.

"What are those?" she said.

I couldn't make eye contact.

"These two are Sazeracs…the other is an Old Fashioned."

"Oh."

The barkeep returned my card and brusquely handed me a receipt with a pen. "What will you be having?" He looked at her.

She squinted at the armory of different whiskeys behind him. I was about to sign the receipt when I caught the listless shifting of her weight. The burly man leered, taut.

"She'll have a Sazerac," I said.

The barkeep nodded. He didn't wait for her answer.

"And yes, I know you were waiting for me to do that. That's what you do, right? You should be ashamed of yourself—hopefully as ashamed as I am for giving in."

"I didn't want you to buy me a drink," she said.

"I didn't want to buy you a drink, either."

"Then, why did you?"

"Because that was awkward."

She blinked. "What?"

"He was waiting. You were all coy." I made my best impression to her amusement. "He looked at me. It was like I was expected to. You know what I'm talking about."

"You're so dumb," she said.

With those last words, I grew excited. I could almost feel the burn of Lucia's eyes. I made a peek around just in case. I was safe; I leaned in.

"You're so dumb."

She laughed.

"I'm Iosef—a movie star," I said gaily.

"Oh, really?"

"Yeah, you don't know me?"

She indulged in a taste of one of my Sazeracs. Already I felt my extremities warm and my heart pound on the inside of my ribcage. Further in I leaned—and I am sure all of my intentions were alive and naked. The barkeep returned and threw down a new bill. We didn't skip a beat.

"Nope," she said.

"Then that's your problem."

She gesticulated, as if to retort, but stopped short. She blinked again, at a loss.

"I'm Anaïs." She lightly touched my hand before I could sign. "Please, let me."

For the first time, perhaps because it had been loud and the conversation, trifling, I recognized the French angel wafting about the pronunciation of her words. She gave me a devious look. I relinquished the pen. Quickly, she wrote in a generous tip and signed my name. To top it off she put a heart next to the signature. The barkeep swooped it up without thought.

I stared at her daftly. She guffawed.

And off she was with a twinkle of bravado.

For the rest of the night, I was in a daze. Lucia and Borges entertained me with chatter, and I of course participated, but I could not remember. Every so often, like a revenant lost, I would search for the face of my salvation in every passing tramp. Everyone noticed. Lucia, Borges, the succubae—I even noticed.

Anaïs stayed to the back of the patio. Three times she caught me staring—and not once did she acknowledge me. My attention would flee, I would feign innocence—and perhaps, I ever so wished, before she *could* smile. I supposed I'd never know. The last time, however, was not of my accord. I heard her guffaw again. I looked before I could even think about it. Purely, it was a visceral reaction, the kind that educated me in regards to my subtle natures. I saw the criminal lifting of the douche lord's mustache. She stood beside him, close. She touched his hand and continued to guffaw, and in just the manner that she had guffawed with me. Her laugh flattened a note once she noticed me and I felt creepy.

"Listen. This is what I'm saying. The Occupy Movement is a huge leap forward in many cases. The anti-war movement has died out, and although war is still happening. Inequality continues to get worse, people have lost their homes, their jobs, and their lives, really, since no one can live the way that they used to live. So, what I'm trying to say is that while conditions in this alleged United States of America are continuously worsening, there has been no good movement in terms of actual resistance. So when the Occupy Movement started, it really corrected for this, and I agree, it has absolutely changed the dialogue."

Lucia gesticulated to preempt Borges interruption and continued fervently.

"That said—let's look at the negative side, because there are always weaknesses to everything, yes? And it isn't necessarily bad to point these out. If done properly, only through this sort of criticism can things progress for once. Anyway, the criticisms are true. There is no leadership. You saw it when we were at the last meeting. It was chaos. Nothing got accomplished. We had an agenda of five things—five things only, for fuck's sake. And we only made it to the second item, which was the location of the next meeting, the first being the name of the god damned meeting. Everyone is being too liberal and weird and trying to allow absolute equality and care to every deranged and stupid person. There needs to be leadership—"

"There was leadership," Borges said.

"Yeah, you're right, there was…although there wasn't supposed to be any, which means they have their heads up their asses, too," she said.

"Calm down," he said. "What are you trying to say? You want them to have leaders or not, which one is it?"

"You're an idiot. All I was doing was pointing out that, as you just recognized, the movement has contradictions, even one as base as that, but no one wants to recognize them. Of course I think they need leadership. I think they just need good leadership."

"Iosef?" Borges said.

"Pay attention. Stop being so god damned blah. We're having an important conversation," Lucia said to me.

She reached over and hit me. My whiskey splashed, and only then did she continue.

"Here is all that I am saying. They need central leadership. The movement ultimately needs a body of individuals, elected and monitored by the people involved in the movement, in some manner of organization, I don't care what it's called, party or what, that can make the best informed and educated decisions possible for the moment when idealist democracy and complexity are paralyzing." She held up a finger to stave off Borges irreconcilable annoyance at her long-windedness. "Additionally, I am saying that the movement is lacking in a motivating ideology. So far, it's a litany of complaints directed at inequality and the domination of the one percent, but what do we want? What is the goal? The problems are clearly systemic, so unless the root of the problem is addressed, then the same things are doomed to repeat, making this resistance worthless—especially since history has already given us enough examples to learn from. I mean, look, earlier generations fought for the welfare state, unions, and not for revolution, and look where we're at? All those gains are being lost. So, what I'm saying—"

"Question," Borges said.

"Yah, yah, what?"

"—For comrade Iosef," he said, ignoring her grumbles. "What's the problem with central leadership—with authority? —and can you also respond to Ms. Stalina's apparent reference towards the revolution of the socialist or communist tragedy?"

He held an invisible microphone to my face and sipped his Sazerac, the same one Anaïs sipped. I couldn't stop thinking about her, or how I was appearing. Having been forced to perk up, I acquiesced to his attention. First, though, I took a stiff drink of my Old Fashioned to allow for the gathering of my scattered thoughts.

"Look, I'm tired—"

"You're always tired," Lucia said.

"God, will you shut up," I said.

At once, I experienced a new wind. Peripherally, I knew that Qandisa could be watching. Consequently, I imagined how I should look. This was my chance, I thought to myself. And thus, I let my imagination be.

"Take this heuristically," I said. "It has generally been noted that there are three 'stages' of the development of human cognition—concrete, formal, and post-formal. Concrete thinking lacks in abstractness; it is dominated by the motif of naïve empiricism, although, philosophically, Hegel would have argued that it is the *most* abstract form of thought, I think— actually, I don't know. Already, I digress—I'm sorry—anyway, a concrete thinker, like most children, will only be able to give you a literal reading of a proverb. My drink is red. Ask them what this means with a wry smile and they'll tell you, 'It's a red drink.' Formal thinking is defined by the heaviness of basic abstraction. Teenagers and young adults are often in this developmental stage of cognition, they think in terms of categories and principles as if they are literal and real. They are very black and white with their reasoning. 'You are democratic, as defined by the principle of listening and considering other peoples' views non-tyrannically; however, I just saw you shut that person down; that is the opposite of democracy; you are not a democrat!' In teenagers and young adults, this level of cognition is represented by their propensity to point out hypocrisy with little insight. Tell them a proverb, they'll read into its universal meaning, but they'll reify this meaning as absolute and a literal measure of one-dimensional truth. Post-formal cognition allegedly represents an attenuated ability to reason and navigate through those boggling shades of gray—or in short, to utilize human reason more contextually and fluidly in all universes, once again in concert with the facts, including those of signification and perception."

Borges looked perplexed.

"Ok, professor." He maintained his invisible microphone with feigned fatigue and a mischievous grin. "Please continue."

"Never mind," I said.

"No, no. Continue. You're just too long-winded," Lucia said.

"Ha. *Lucia* thinks you're long-winded."

"Bah," I said.

"Come on," he said.

"Yeah, come on," Lucia said, "stop being a little bitch."

"It's hard to be concise," I said, having to fight down the most horrid and malevolent of feelings. I positioned myself as wittily and as amicably as I could muster. "I wouldn't expect the..., well, minds of a certain quality...to you know...be able to appreciate the requisites of any real exploration."

"Uh huh," Lucia said. "Of a certain quality. Go ahead."

"Let the man finish. I want to go for another drink one of these days."

"Ok, ok. My point is this. We have all accepted one axiomatic proposition, even the radicals—the unevenness of development, of dispositions, and characteristics is organic, inevitable, really…what's the word…insurmountable. Well, for the purposes of this conversation, what is authority?—It is a *state* of power—to be able to determine the relations of things—and this power is at least partially constituted by beliefs. And even the most erudite of ideas, and of their systems, ideologies, are in essence only quasi-dimensional. Follow the algorithm that must follow from this. If the world is irreducibly complex and composed of differences just as much as similarities, then any idea is essentially a bulldozer. Is not violence, therefore, intrinsic?"

Lucia leaned forward to disagree. I started talking again.

"There is no such thing as a non-violent revolution—or a peaceful leader. This is a contradiction in terms. Modern progressives are faced with a choice. Respect differences and live authentically, at least spiritually in some ways—or destroy them—for the sake of a vision—and thereby live authentically in others. Postmodernism is not a game stopper. All it did was draw attention to the will in the equation."

I simpered, appearing pleased, unsure of whether I had made my point.

"So, Lucia, stop being afraid of your own agency," I said.

"I'm not afraid."

"I'm sorry—I misspoke—stop being ashamed. Stop hiding behind democratic phraseology and just accept that, deep down, you pine to be a butcher so that you can carry forward naturally—unhindered by the consciences of weaker human beings."

Borges hee-hawed.

"What kind of therapist are you?" he said.

I took a pensive moment.

"One who is destined for greatness," I responded.

I raised my drink. The jubilant tone of my voice, which contradicted the wry and cynical expression that I could feel on my face, produced a boggled look on the bearings of my companions. After an extended moment of silence, they both burst into a hysterical laughter.

Lucia turned red and couldn't stop. She even almost tipped her drink.

Borges gasped for breath. "You're fucking crazy," he said, holding his stomach, "Oh, man."

And at that moment I again caught a glimpse of Anaïs. She saw me laughing. I guess I was laughing with them. It was true—she had indeed been watching. She smiled. And I did too. I felt well.

CHAPTER SIX

I

When Napoleon arrived to the office, he did so with imperial flare. The agency driver scooted in before him, his eyes wide with excitement and fear. He hastily made a few warning gestures my way before becoming terribly self-conscious. Gigante caught the closing sweep of the door, commanded it open again, pivoted crisply towards me after surveying the scene, and finally marched inside with an emperor's practiced stride. The driver fled without further ado. I leaned over to peek outside. All the other clients were clustered together, busy with gossip. They stayed away.

"Good morning, Napoleon," I said, a bit too merry.

"You will not address me by my given name."

The tone of his voice was pompous, impatient. I did not detect the slightest crack or second-guessing in its articulation. I nodded, finding no words.

"I'm ready to address you and your people," he said. He closed in on my personal space, dwarfing me. He glared down with an irascible gaze.

"Right this way," I said.

As I walked towards my office door, I did so quickly and with my head askew so that I could have a sense of him peripherally. He acquiesced to my lead and trailed me with his arms regally folded in a perpendicular fashion. One of his hands curled into a fist to rest his chin as he strode.

I opened the door for him and humbly beseeched his entrance. Assiduously, I searched his person to assess for weapons and the extent of his psychosis. He dressed in black jeans and what appeared to be the ruffled gothic red shirt of a Halloween costume. Over this, he wore a long black pea coat that draped his figure. All of this clothing appeared drab, dirty, littered by cat hair. Decomposing rubber soles and what appeared to be smears of sticky lint similarly tarnished his dress shoes. I wondered what he had in his pockets. I made note of bulges.

His saffron cheeks, mostly lacking in the usual dark pigment, appeared with a feverish glow, obtusely matching the uneven terrain of his slick obsidian bed-head. All I could smell was his odor; it affronted with scents of must and spoilage. He lingered ominously. His eyes were electrified.

"I am here to address the people—I know what has been happening—the clarity has reached its indivisible degree of brightness.—I have been informed of what's going on—the great end, the Savior—I am the Savior—you know this, and my demands—I have come to have them filled—Yes, yes?—…"

He addressed something floating above him.

"—Y-Yes, I'll tell them…"

He was short-tempered but momentarily respectful with his interlocutor.

"—I will not ask for too much, just what I need to accomplish the Great Purification—to ask for any more or less would be a travesty—all enemies of the Great Purification, of the Savior—," he glared at me, "—I-I am the Savior—will be raped by dark light—but not evil light, I am sorry, no, no, no—not evil light—the combination, cosmically, of dark matter, invisible matter, and rays of light traveling at a thousand percent clarity and speed—Yes."

He experienced a paroxysm.

"Napol—I'm sorry," I stammered. "What can I do for you today? —Actually, I'm glad you're here. We need to talk."

"Yes."

"I've been trying to reach you. I visited your house a few times you know. We were going to have to go forward with graduating you from the program since we hadn't been able to contact you."

"No, no, nothing of this sort will be done—I am here because I have been wronged greatly by this program and don't you think for a second that I don't know who you guys are. Yes."

He touched his thumbs and forefingers together into a symbol of an eye, or a pyramid.

"I don't know what that means." I paused. "I'm sorry."

"I am a King...the Emperor of this hemisphere. I am the Savior and Lord. And you very well know what this means, don't you patronize me."

Paul pushed the door open further; he peeked in and pretended to only accidentally disturb us.

"Oh. You guys need anything?" He looked at me pointedly after acknowledging the imperious figure of the Emperor with a clueless nod.

"Yes, in fact," I said. "As you can see, we have a visitor, and he is to be taken *very* seriously. He is proclaiming that he has been wronged and—," I looked at Napoleon with a humble affection, "—if I may so assume, is here for such wrongs to be justified."

"Yes, I am not leaving until my demands have been received. I am ready to meet with *them*."

"Them?" Paul looked at me again quickly.

Napoleon flashed his hand sign.

"Oh," he said. His expression was empty.

"I will meet with your leaders to start my negotiations. I know they are of the dark. I know they are of the jinn, the daemons, the sprites, the aliens, the serpents—Don't think that I am a fool. I am the next Savior for the Great Purification, and don't think that just because I am of God's light, that I am Jesus, that I am God divisible into one-in-three, or one-from-three, I am sorry, I am tired, this war has been so draining— That I cannot bend the darkness to my use, refracting it 180 degrees so that it indeed might be malevolent light for your punishment, your rape, your saving...yes."

"Can you look for Dr. Weisman, see if he is here? And Mr. Giuseppe," I said.

"The doctor just arrived. Mr. Giuseppe isn't here yet," Paul said.

"I am not leaving until I speak to them both. I know who Francisco is. I know that he is a general of the abyss, that he is a jinn who turned from God to serve the daemons—and thus became a demon. I did not threaten to kill anyone! Anyone! To kill is to eradicate, and I would never do this—That is stupid. Don't you remember what I stand for? —I stand for purification, through torture, through *blessing*. Killing is not what I do—well I do, if I have too—but I haven't had to yet and only rapists and daemons are deserving of this, well daemons that are not or can never be of the light of the Purification..."

Napoleon seemed to experience another orgasmic tremor, and immediately, he conversed with his saints. Paul didn't wait. He took leave.

"Yes, yes...I understand...I shouldn't be too harsh or greedy, I am King, this does not befit me...yes, yes, I will have mercy...yes."

For half a minute there was silence. I lingered there un-surely as the King ominously positioned himself, his arms once again locked in regal fashion. Although he did not speak, I could see his lips moving subtly and rapidly. His eyes remained manic and vocal enough.

I shuffled listlessly, taking extraneous note. Napoleon stood more aggressively. I cringed.

"Alright, so Paul went to find Dr. Weisman. We'll then have a meeting. We are going to do our best to ensure that you receive only the most just of treatments for these circumstances, ok? —I mean, well, you know what I mean. Let me go and postpone group in the meantime."

"I will address the people while I wait." He pulled out a pad of yellow paper and a pen and started scribbling. "Gather them."

Sweat gathered at the brim of my scalp and brow became despotic. Gruesomely, I wiped it away but with all the cover of a dedicated and pressured pensiveness. How was I going to fix this? The situation was going from dangerous to catastrophic.

"I have an idea. I understand that you feel like you have been profoundly wronged," I said.

His eyes went ablaze.

"No, no," I said quickly. "I misspoke. You have to understand, I am only your therapist, I make no major decisions in this agency, so it really is outside of my control what Dr. Weisman or Mr. Giuseppe, or even all our bosses, say—but I know that you want to express your grievance, and you should, you have every right to do so—so follow me, if you wish of course—and allow me to give you the proper paperwork to fill out. This is the process we have to go through, and we'll save time."

I had never thanked God so deeply. He nodded, appeased. And I'll never forget that moment when my voice, which soothed, emerged so pristinely, so organically tranquil from the fiery crag of my core. In fact, it was like it was someone else's voice, like I too was listening to some *other*, some third party eerily present, even as I felt that it was my lips that moved.

II

Paul had called the police. This was the first thing I heard amidst the raucous of whispers at the receptionist's desk. With the Emperor close in tow, I called Marian over to us. She looked at me grimly. Her affect couldn't remain stoic as she glanced upon Napoleon. She tried to smile, but it emerged as a grimace. I informed her of the King's request for a grievance form as he crowded my shoulder.

"Sure. Follow me, Napoleon," she said.

I winced.

He didn't react.

"Be sure to fill that out on the desk, too—we don't want the form to be compromised since its official," I said quickly.

I pointed to the island beside the receptionist desk, which also had a phone, usually for the clients to use. Napoleon nodded.

That's when I caught wind of Dr. Weisman, who was patiently waiting for me beside Paul at the conference room. He waved a file in his hand playfully.

"Crisis, huh?" a client said. He was one from Heidi's load.

"Another one's going crazy," one of Paul's added. I knew his name then, although now I could not recall it.

"Great, this means we're not going to have group," another said.

I turned to the haggard, war-weathered source of the last cranky lament.

"I'm sorry, but you know how it goes. We have to deal with something that popped up unexpectedly. I know it's inconvenient. We can have Marian do this group in a little bit, and I'll resume next week."

"I look forward to these groups and if they're not going to happen we should know so we can prepare for it. It's not fair.

59

If you say group's going to happen at a certain time, then it should. We ain't paying you for nothing!"

"This is a free program for you," I said.

Heidi's client started to chortle snidely, taking great pleasure in the exchange. Paul's joined in.

"I'm sorry. Marian will be with you guys in a bit," I said.

"Great. Now, what's group going to be about? She doesn't even know what we've been talking about."

My cheeks were boiling. I could feel them ache and burn. Again my brow was heavy, and now, my cranium pounded.

I rushed over to the conference room without another word. I greeted the doctor, followed him inside, waited for Paul, and shut the door with brunt gusto.

III

After briefing the doctor on only the details, my spirit capsized in enough panic and guilt to flood my speech with the precursor to sobs. I had to profess my responsibility for the matter; it weighed so much on me and they would be thinking it anyway. "This is my fault," I said in defeat, "I went to visit him but I didn't really try hard enough to keep him medication compliant, especially after his 5150."

The doctor looked at me with reassured airs. He didn't seem to make note of my emotion, which informed me that he had in fact noticed.

"Please. Mr. Gigante is an impaired man. I wouldn't go as far, yet, to say that he meets LPS criteria. He is forwardly psychotic but he has control over his faculties. He is capable of choice and he is *choosing* to be incompliant with treatment. You have no control over that. This man is not FSP material."

I nodded. With muster, I could only bring myself to make the scantest of eye contact. Glossiness, I was certain, had appeared in my eyes. A piss-warm flush of shame washed over me.

"Giuseppe isn't going to be in for another hour or so," Paul said. "I spoke with him. The police should be on their way. This is what we'll do. Let's get him in here and occupy him while we wait for the police. Perhaps we can de-escalate him and we won't even need them." He looked at me and acknowledged my agreement. "Ready doc?"

"Always. But be prepared. You can't trust these guys. Don't block yourselves in. The last thing we need is a turkey shoot."

We heard his commotion outside and realized that the staff and clientele had all gone silent. After one final corroborating exchange, I jolted up and briskly walked towards the lobby.

"I am here for justice. I know you know who I am, and I *will* be heard."

Again, Gigante foreboded the symbol of his quivering phalanges.

"What does that mean?" said Dr. Weisman.

"You know what it means."

"Let's assume I did—or I thought I did. However, I need to hear it from you."

"It is the sign of the one percent of the one percent; it is the signifier of the metaphysical elite. A sign that is at once eye and pyramid."

He finished his explanation with a nonsensical phrase in what seemed like butchered Latin.

"Who am I?" the doctor asked.

"You are jinn."

"...Jinn?" I said. "I think I know what that is, but could you also explain it? I'm sorry if this sounds immaterial to you. I'm just trying to learn."

"Of course, you wouldn't know, there is no reason you should know, or need to know, I only found out at the beginning of my transformation when my 'psychosis' began, my purification. A jinn was one of the races of God, a magical race of beings, magical, telepathic, mostly superior to humankind. Like humans, they do not have to serve the Light, but yes, they are superior, and because of this, sometimes nasty beings that take many shapes. Many jinn serve the daemons or have become daemons themselves, beings of a higher degree of clarity and power in the cosmos thinking that they approach God but do not."

Napoleon fixated on the doctor.

"I know about you. You slaughtered five thousand men in Persia before it was Iran. You have earned your title as a lesser general of the one percent mystic godlings. Surely you must recognize me too for who I truly am. I saved millions a decade ago through the use of my powers, respect is due. When the Great False Purifications happened, my spirit in another alternate manifestation helped to bring the imperialistic false avatar of the Dark-Light down. I again did this time again. But oh, you wait Jinn, the real, the true, the pure Great Purification is coming by the New Year." He paused. "I must prepare. You can still be saved."

"You're very intelligent," Dr. Weisman said. "You're brilliant. You have an understanding of metaphysics and science, of history, of the essences of things, well beyond what the average mind can comprehend. In fact, I would say that your thoughts move so fast, and are so sweeping in profundity, that others aren't capable of understanding you at all. This must be frustrating since you have a purpose."

Napoleon appeared to partially seize. His neck jerked and his face contorted as he experienced another paroxysm of wide-eyed whispers. His mouth wretched open so far askew and so gruffly that I thought he could have mashed his teeth.

He replicated a sequence of gagging-like noises as he continued to shake and whisper in spurts, hands out turned in prayer.

"Oh, I do apologize. When the spirits communicate with me, they try to speak through me. It is rather embarrassing. Yes."

"That's alright," the doctor said. "I understand. What was just communicating with you?"

"Just a reiteration of the cosmic laws and the manifestation of my coming godhood. I am still undergoing my great purification."

"Cosmic laws? Can you explain these to us?"

"Yes."

Napoleon's throat convulsed as he attempted to swallow and breathe at the same time. He looked nervous, now. But in a shift, he became confident again. With new self-assurance, he calmly stood from his chair, knocking it back with his mechanical motions. The clash of it re-startled him. He looked confused then walked over to a dry erase board that we never used for meetings.

"I am still in process. My visions cannot be considered *completely* accurate. This you must understand."

He drew a series of red dots with a marker he carefully chose.

"It is also impossible to communicate the degree of lucidity, of clarity, the truthful essence of this truth. But you will have to stretch your minds."

He connected the dots with jagged, impetuously drawn lines. When he finished, there was a vagueness to its structure.

"Development is never straight like a line, but rather back and forth, up and down, to the point where, although it is indeed a process with a direction, it appears like it is chaos. There has never been a beginning to time, but then, yes, yes, there was a beginning, and this beginning is *in* its non-beginning. God burst forth, the One, he/she/it, otherwise known as The, Object, Thing, Eternity, Nothing, Everything, All, One, and so forth; and from this point of singularity, One/All morphed, burst, gave mediation through its destruction, to everything/all things/all beings. Don't get me wrong, this is night, I mean, not, a nature/nurture, god/science debate—no, no, no, evolution exists as a force-directional starting from this point of pointlessness."

He ensured our attention. He had an overly vibrant and paternalistic expression with his chin dipped inward and his eyebrows raised.

"From here, as the good book says, not the Bible, but the Quran, the jinn, the humans, daemons, demons, and all beings came into existence from the One. Many races were born or came to be and passed. Only *I* know this. And yes, the books must all be read like one chapter to one larger book, as a sort of relational-contradictory and, therefore, the signification of essences. And once every few thousand years," he gestured towards his sketch, "the One manifests itself after gathering a greater proportion, or degree, of its essence into a new step towards the singularity. These are all those, such as Tupac Amaru, Jesus Christ, Moses, Mohammed, up to some of the Popes, etc. It is controversial, I know, but sometimes there can be two manifestations, uneven that is, of the singularity but as different proportionalities or parts of the essences."

He didn't even appear in need of breath. I felt dizzy trying to follow him.

"Time is not linear. Linearity is an illusion, a lie. It is thought blocking like I have been thought blocked—but all thoughts will be unblocked as I move towards purification. Time can be traveled backward too, but this has yet to be accomplished—I might do it, but only after my great purification. I used to be Napoleon Gigante, that was my former dirty, sinful self, that was not yet at a degree of clarity-insanity as I am now, closer to the singularity—experts have even noted that I could be the purest form of the singularity yet. Which is why the jinn and devils thought to block me—But I cannot be blocked forever! No!"

He laughed.

"Do you not see, now? With the capacitor, which I am re-inventing from the messages relayed to me by my selves through film, I can travel back after attaining the ninetieth degree of pure consciousness to revolutionize the self through the gathering of the singularity. I will achieve this ability by the New Year, which will begin the Great Purification where all my estrangement will be destroyed/reincorporated into the totality of the One."

He again took note of our dispositions. He shook his head.

"I'll stop there." He whispered to the right and adopted a tinge of humility. "Yes, yes, I know I have told much, but they must be punished."

"That's a lot," the doctor said. "Just give me a second."

He made some scribbles and exchanged a look with us.

"You just went from the nature of time and space and existence to the dynamism between the Spirit and our material selves, to time travel, purities of consciousness...I had to write it down quickly. I cannot even grasp it, really."

"Yes," Napoleon said with a self-congratulatory smirk.

"Your awareness is so rich, so deep, that it really is hard to fathom. You've come to this agency for a purpose, yes?"

"I will have justice! Yes."

"You have a message to deliver to the people, am I right? I think you came to me because you wanted myself and your therapist to assist you. Right now, Napoleon, you're experiencing what is called a flight of ideas again—in case you forgot, that means that you think so mercurially that it actually impairs your ability to communicate with others since they are not as prodigious. Remember, this has happened before. I've also heard a lot of this before and it didn't end well. It ended in hospitalization. From here."

Napoleon became viscerally suspicious.

"Because I respect you, I'm going to get to the point. You're not taking your medication. Are you feeling depressed, anxious?"

"I am not depressed! I have never felt so perfect."

"Ok, ok."

"I am a little anxious, though—yes—but the medication makes it worse. I take the Zyprexa, and then I feel too anxious. I do not need it, I am better without it."

"Now, don't lie to yourself. You're too brilliant and too important for that. You have a purpose on this earth. And just the fact that you're here today tells me that you are seeking our assistance so we can empower you to succeed further. When I first met you, you told me you were on your way to purification, and you called me your guardian in this quest. Is this not true?"

Reluctantly, he nodded.

"Your message has not gotten out there. And this is because you're gravely impaired, Napoleon. By taking your medication, you will retain all your intelligence, but you will also achieve more clarity. You will actually be able to communicate your thoughts in a manner that will help you succeed."

"I take my medication that helps me sleep. But I have not been able to sleep."

"I can see that. You have all the features of someone who isn't sleeping."

He paused, careful.

"Will you allow me to administer a shot of your Zyprexa?"

"No, it makes me anxious."

The doctor tapped his own forehead, slowly.

"This is what is making you anxious. The medication doesn't cause anxiety."

I hadn't appreciated Napoleon's slight grounding to reality until the volatile jolt of his frustration clamorously re-triggered his aggressive affect. In one loud shift, all the murderous electricity in his eyes returned. It was the same look that he possessed when we had to 5150 him the first time.

"I will have my justice!"

He slammed his fist on the table.

"You took your medication for months before you stopped." The doctor didn't respond to Napoleon's antics. "You felt better, remember? It didn't cause you anxiety then."

Napoleon shoved his grievance papers forward into the air. He murmured something. Neither Paul nor I heard it, but the doctor swore that it was an oath to purify us through force.

That's when the police arrived. Napoleon immediately signaled his divine sign for their subservience. "Arrest them. They have made false proportions. I require justice."

A female officer commanded him to put his hands behind his back. A male officer behind her had his hand on his holster. Without resistance, Napoleon did as he was told. "I am the One," he said. They patted him down and searched his pockets. They found a black plastic pen on him, which appeared to have blood on it. They asked him about it. He said that he had to sketch his prophecies.

Of course, when they asked him if he had any intention of harming anyone, he denied it. His affect became terrible in its tranquility. After speaking with us shortly to corroborate our statements, the police asked us if we wanted to press criminal charges concerning alleged 'terrorist threats,' although this didn't quite seem appropriate due to his mental state. We said that we didn't. They became extremely bored with us. Napoleon was told that he was not to visit our premises without our permission. It turned out that the driver hadn't even transported him. This had only appeared to be the case since, by coincidence, they had all arrived at the same time. I had been trying to discharge him, somewhat dishonestly, so I never would have instructed the driver to pick him up. In fact, I was going to reprimand the driver, thinking that he had picked up Gigante on his own, but then I found out that he had nothing to do with it.

Napoleon agreed to return to the clinic solely with our permission and to take his Zyprexa. He gave each of us a fervent acknowledgment, which appeared to me as spurious. He pointed to his grievance papers with wild eyes. And then he left with the police officers to be taken to the nearest bus stop, the one from which he came.

Mr. Giuseppe arrived shortly after as if he had planned, and ever so perfectly, to avoid all involvement and responsibility. Paul filled him in. Collectively, we came up with a plan. Talk to his mother, educate her on the importance of ensuring his medication compliance, Napoleon's need for a higher level of care, on meetings with the DMH coordinators, etc., etc. At that point, I didn't care. I was asked to repeat it all and I couldn't. I warranted strange looks. When I got back to my office, I cried. Paul comforted me.

CHAPTER SEVEN

I

Around the office, I was a star for the next couple weeks. People, in general, were vibrant after the crisis. Vibrancy is the best word, although it is an awkward one—I cannot categorize the spirit as wholly terrified or excited. It was a strange intimacy of both. Regardless, their affects were quite alive where formerly they had been empty.

Jolie even looked more energetic. Usually, her neurotic sexuality conjoined with a strange necrotic presence, as if beneath her glamor of paints and perfumes there rotted an abscess. I always imagined that casual sex with younger men at bars on the weekends was the single recurrent phenomenon responsible for her ability to move. She remained hyper vigilant, ever so chatty, but now she was genuinely more friendly with me. For the first time ever, I also found her alluring.

Marian, Mr. Giuseppe, Dr. Weisman, and all the nameless staffers, even Heidi—they all interacted with me differently after that point. My words were accepted with reverence. More, they were even solicited, and this had never been the case. Strange, this psychology—as I gained in capital, I found myself liking others more as well. Except for Heidi. Before I was more curious about her, even attracted. The more she exchanged all the subtle niceties of warmth with Paul, the more I felt unwanted, the more I wanted to talk with her and to know her, to explore her clinical culture and inside world. But now? Now that she was curious of me? I found myself *reviled*. This schema, again, struck me as frivolous, and I suffered for it.

Things hadn't improved with Napoleon. Since his visit, he called the agency at least three times a day. He texted threats about my torture and rape to my work phone. He directed me to his Instagram profile. In one picture, he was holding a rifle, but the picture was old. There were declarations there too— and each them followed by hundreds of comments—all of them his own. "There will be justice! The Great Purification approaches!"

I traveled to his home once during this period. To all of our surprise, he had followed through and taken his medications for a few days. His mother confirmed this. My clinical sense informed me that this was not enough time for the drug to reach effective levels in his system, but he did seem to improve quickly for some reason. Perhaps it was just from sleep.

At any rate, Paul accompanied me. We spoke to his mother about the importance of a structured schedule for Napoleon. For example, we told her to help him take his medications on time and stay busy with positive activities that helped to regulate his stress, anxiety, and depression.

She mostly spoke Spanish and was thinned out, emotionally. Other children lived in the home, including her adult daughter, Cassandra. She worried about their safety. Napoleon often paced and punched holes in the walls while giving seemingly nonsensical monologues and capricious displays of affection and rage. For two hours, she cried as she detailed a narrative where Napoleon served both as Pontius and as the object of crucifixion. His stepfather abused him. Over the years, she said, Napoleon had been subjected to her unstable relationships, which often times included the flagrant abuse of alcohol and drugs in an openly promiscuous environment. Things were different now; she cleaned up, worked hard, found the Lord.

And so did he. Ever since his late teens, though, and especially after his later years in the university, he had been behaving very eccentrically. He also had a drug habit, his mother alleged—Napoleon was fond of marijuana and amphetamine.

During this visit, Paul looked as edgy as I felt. My imagination supplied visions of the Emperor emerging from the back of the house with his rifle. As paranoid and morbid as my imagination proved to be, this never happened. He peeked out, meekly—but before anyone could say anything, he made skittish retreat like a punished child. The same ensemble of clothes coroneted his shoulders, except they looked much more soiled and unkempt.

We promised to be in touch the following week. After supplying our work numbers to her, we also gave her the crisis line number again, which one of us always possessed since, as per the county policy, FSP programs had to be accessible 24 hours a day for emergencies.

II

"Hey, Lenore," I said.

As I entered her home, I took note of a distinctly new smell. I paused and analyzed it to her bemusement.

"Are you cooking?" I said.

"Yeah, make yourself at home. Want a drink of water?"

"No thank you. Food?"

"No, I'm cooking meth."

She waddled into the kitchen area. I tried my best to sneak a look. She had two pots steaming. I recognized the smell of rice and simmering beef.

She sat down again, a little closer to me than usual. For the first time, I noticed that she was wearing makeup. She seemed thinner. Although my suspicions became aroused, I took the time to appreciate that her pupils were properly constricted.

"You're looking great," I said.

"Surprised? Oh. Here…" She supplied to me a few sheets of paper with wily scribbles after fetching them from a nearby cluttered desktop. "I don't know if it is what you were looking for," her voice trembled slightly, embarrassed, "…but…well…I did what I thought you wanted me to do as I understood it."

"Oh, wow." I stopped to search for words. "This is wonderful." I read them in a cursory fashion. "You did some exploration. This is truly wonderful. Well, before we go over them, let's check in. You weren't feeling this before. What's changed?"

"Well, after you left last time, I couldn't stop thinking about our conversation. I guess it bothered me. No, not you, you didn't do anything wrong. It's just, you don't really understand, you can't, we've all been in this program a long time. We've seen three different directors and…" She stopped to count, "…three, four…five—no! -Six therapists. Well, I've seen six different therapists. I've had one therapist for as long as you, but all the others, I only had for a minute before they were gone."

"I don't think I can really appreciate that process," I said.

"So, I don't know, it's like…why even try? Why even tell the person all about yourself, go through all those things, if they're not even going to be there long, and the next one will want you to do the same and even tell you to do the same things," she said. "Poor babies. You're stuck with clients like us."

"And here I am, bumbling in, thinking I'm so skillful when in fact, I have been doing everything that has already been done, and probably better, by others. You're probably a more experienced therapist than me."

She nudged me. I laughed, tense.

"Yep." She looked away for a few seconds. "No, no…you've been really helpful."

"I don't know what I've done to be helpful."

"You've stuck with me."

"So," I paused. "I've just existed."

"You've helped me to think."

I re-read her journal papers. She hurried to walk into the kitchen to fuss with the cooking. "Sure you don't want anything? It's almost done."

"You know my answer. I totally wish I could, but it's policy. We can't accept that sort of stuff."

"Yeah, and once you accept some rice con carne, you never know what could happen next."

I turned red.

Faintly, Lenore chuckled again through the clinks of utensils and the simmering of boiled rice. The aroma of the food became even more diffuse throughout her apartment. It smelled delicious. I was reminded of my youth, when I would sit on the carpet and draw as I watched afternoon cartoons after school as my mother prepared dinner. A memory of her garrulous nature on the phone also returned, and I felt the slightest prick of anxiety.

Lenore had returned from her tending. She smiled—but this time, her expression was very genuine and sweet. I realized I had been staring vacantly at the table with her journal papers in my hand. I laughed lowly and apologized.

"I realized that I was stuck in the same pattern," she said. "I just can't shake this feeling, you know, the 'blah' feeling. I'm always feeling tired," she had started to rearrange the crumpled papers, letterheads, and scraps on the table, "...I'm always feeling down. I don't even know if it's really sadness, but it sort of is. I can't even think straight, either, because I'm always in pain—you know, my neck, shoulders. Anyway, I realized that I never do the proper thing for my kids, like make them breakfast, I never seem happy...I just wake up, snap at them and tell them to go get some cereal before I drag myself up

73

from bed. I take them to school and then I would just sleep." She looked away. "I just feel so guilty."

Quietly, I held the space.

"So I finally tried something different, although it was a pain. I forced myself to wake up an hour earlier than usual in order to give me extra time to snooze and get done being cranky. This was last week. Then I made eggs and toast. I also forced myself to stay awake after dropping them off. I've been trying to get into the habit of using that time to do chores and, you know, to do all my motherly responsibilities. Oh, why is life so miserable?..."

Lenore finally started to weep. I could not comfort her, although I wanted to. However, I was there—and this presence, I would hope, seemed empathic. I realized that my eyes stung again. They were dry, I think, or it could have been that I wanted to help her so bad. We worked out a predictable clinical plan. She was to continue with her behavioral modifications, remain medication compliant, avoid old friends who used methamphetamine, and continue journaling. But I couldn't help but notice that the manner in which she forsook her past was reminiscent of the sophomoric mourner who fervently made the oath to disinherit all wounds.

III

When I got back to the office I made absolutely no effort to socialize. Jolie was scoffing into the phone, leaning back in her chair in her typical bothered fashion. The lobby was full of intakes impatient, desperate, or blunted in affect. Mr. Giuseppe acknowledged me with a pressured smile as he scooted across the building with papers in his hand. As I approached my office, I saw that he beckoned for Marian before entering Paul's.

Heidi was working at her desk.

"Have a second?" She looked troubled.

"Not really, have to start working on my notes."

"Alright."

I had started to type when I realized that, between my strokes, there was no sound of a clicking keyboard from her desk. I looked over at her.

"Oh, no," she said, prissily, "don't worry, go back to your deep reflections. I know your cases are so important."

"Ok," I said.

I bobbed my head back and forth in a nonsensical and sarcastic fashion before turning back towards my desk. But after a moment, I kicked off and rolled over to her station.

"Fine. Show me."

"Well, I'm working on this assessment and treatment plan, but I don't know how to diagnose this person. You're going to like him."

I motioned for her to go on.

"He's a twenty-four-year-old referred to us from an outpatient clinic from downtown. He reports that he isn't suffering from any clinically significant symptoms of depression—you know, the usual array of things, persistent sadness, feelings of worthlessness, guilt, shame, hopelessness, cognitive impairment, no energy, and so forth. Also, he doesn't report any anxiety. That doesn't mean I can't see the signs of these things, however—he seems generally disinterested and disconnected, his affect was relatively flat, and he fidgeted restlessly and seemed hyper-aware of everything around him."

"Sleep?"

"He was sarcastic. He sort of deflected, but said it was alright."

"How many hours?"

"Five to seven."

I shrugged. "Sounds normal."

"Yeah. I think I definitely noticed some Axis II features—perhaps a little narcissism…" She returned to her thought process. Her face became horribly squished. "Anyway, he basically denies all symptoms. But he's so weird."

"What did the referral say? He meets criteria?"

"Approximately 30 days in jail in the past year for drugs, vandalism, destruction of property, resisting arrest." She didn't conceal her mischief. "And current homelessness with the threat of future homelessness, lack of mental health services." She was stretching the rules to justify treatment.

"But he came from an outpatient, didn't you say that?"

"Yeah, but they only did outreach, too."

My notes started to pound on the back of my head. I became terribly impatient. She must have noticed the ephemeral irritation in my disposition.

"He was referred by a social worker volunteering at the Occupy encampment," she said quickly. "Isn't that so cool? Finally, I get an interesting case. On the referral, it basically says he's underserved and too intense for regular outpatient. He hasn't been homeless for 120 days, about 80 it said, but he isn't allowed to return home. He was referred over with Psychotic NOS."

"He's not mentally ill. He's an anarchist. And he's probably malingering."

"Probably," she shrugged. "And that's why I don't know how to diagnose him. Well, no, he did present with some strange cognitions. But his context makes any judgment hard. He would smirk and say he was a prophet. Talk about power structures limiting him. That he was oppressed. So, it could be grandiosity, delusions of paranoia and persecution, or, it could be ideology. He mentioned that his 'brain doesn't work like other peoples' brains,' but every time I asked for more detail, he would scoff, look away, and offer only some content-less pseudo-philosophical phrase."

"Him personally, or society, et cetera?"

"Him personally."

I gestured dismissively.

"Keep Psychotic NOS. I highly doubt he's important enough for any government repression. You can always change it later."

"What about the treatment plan?"

"Social rehab."

Then I had a dull epiphany.

"Seasonal affective disorder," I said.

Everyone in the mental health field knew that when we used that diagnosis the case wasn't serious. She bounced up and down. I remained reserved at first, but eventually I couldn't help but to join in on the charade.

"I'm going to write in postpartum depression," she said. "You know, from parting from his mom's house." And with that, Heidi giggled and returned to work.

IV

Paul burst into our office.

"You have a minute?"

He looked haggard. He was staring at me, alarmed.

"Yeah, of course."

"We lost a client."

"Who?" Heidi said, sitting up straight.

"Giuseppe wants us to work together to audit her file immediately. DMH is going to be looking it over."

"Who?" she iterated.

I could tell by the shock and apprehension on her face that she was afraid that the client was hers.

"Garcia, Irene," he said.

"Oh," I said.

Heidi gazed at me. She looked to Paul awkwardly. Perhaps she saw the confused, detached look on my face that betrayed the fact that I had not seen her in quite some time, or that I had forgotten about her altogether.

"She slammed heroin after taking all of her pills," Paul said.

"How did we find out?" I said.

"Police found her, checked the integrated system. They called DMH. Now DMH is requesting her file, like, now. Your notes all caught up? Is the file up to date?"

"No." I shrugged, looking past him at the skewed door to the lobby. "I can justify all my billing. I am covered in terms of liability. I have documented mostly everything."

The tranquility of my voice caused me pause. No one said anything. Mr. Giuseppe briskly entered the room. Paul shuffled to the side and rediscovered his proto-managerial deportment. Heidi quickly looked away.

"I want all your notes done and signed in the next hour. I want all the notes printed out. That file will be on my desk by three," Giuseppe said.

Before leaving, he locked eyes with me perilously. Then he was gone.

And for the next hour, I wrote notes. Banal ones, strewn from the obtuse, formal, and absolutely alien language of the clinician, which drew roses with scientific truth procedures and which reduced the supple flesh of its existence to the synthetic seamlessness of the philistine's postmodern sketchbook—and all because I loved to help people, because I loved them.

CHAPTER EIGHT

I

My performance at the Department of Mental Health coordination meeting was almost impeccable. The strings of my words flowed wonderfully, like notes of music from a Baldwin piano. Although far from atypical in clinical format, as my propositions travelled the topography of different axes, they coalesced into one perfect totality, into one medical and psychological portrait of my former client; and of course, as to avoid the denotation of my detachment, I made good use of my naturally occurring anxiety—I commandeered the tremble of my tenor voice for the representation of humanity—for the illusion of empathy, which was requisite for warmth within the overly scholastic display of clinical knowledge.

"Irene Garcia," the head navigator of services said, with heavy eyelids and a matching gravity to her voice. She leaned heavily on her elbows and leaned forward into her stare. "That is the next item on the agenda. This was a difficult case. Mr. Giuseppe has already informed me of some of its details, but I figured it would be a good thing to discuss in case other providers are facing similar situations."

The situation was far from resolved. This was an Inquisition.

"Could you tell us a little about the case?"

"Of course," I said. "Irene Garcia arrived at our agency about seven months ago. She was a thirty-one year old Hispanic female with three children: two boys, aged three and five and one eight-year-old girl—each of them had different fathers, and every one of them had been adopted out, her last only about two months ago following her suicide attempt that preceded this last one."

Mentioning her last suicide attempt, which was so closely situated to her recent success, seemed to strike me as prima facie evidence of my mishandling of the case. However, I knew this was only a fear of mine. I swallowed. Then I recollected myself, sighed somberly and visibly, and recommenced.

"Her Axis I diagnosis was Bipolar Disorder NOS. Mostly, she presented well-groomed with a relatively euthymic affect, although she also demonstrated some expansiveness here and there. She always displayed orientation times four—to space, time, place, and situation—and always spoke logically in appropriate sequences of comprehensible thought and communication. In terms of her thought content, she did show signs of paranoia, but it was always of the non-bizarre quality and never quite categorically psychotic. When she spoke, she did have a propensity towards circumstantial and tangential processes, in addition to hyper-verbosity and pressured speech. However, only once was she symptomatic of a flight of ideas. Ms. Garcia seemed to be of average intelligence, had a good fund of knowledge, an adequate vocabulary, and no detectable impairments in remote, short, or immediate memory. Please, excuse me for my own verbosity, I am only trying to be thorough so that I can get better clinical feedback."

"Oh, no, no…" the navigator said. "Continue. This is good."

I nodded. "She wanted to 'get her life together,' this was her stated long-term goal. In association with this, she reported the following presenting problems: her sadness, her methamphetamine abuse, and the absence of her children. However, of course, as per any clinical process, much else surfaced during the assessment. Although she complained about her sadness, tiredness, sleeplessness, and restlessness as her symptoms, I noted many signs of mania—and in her case hypomania— some of which I already mentioned. However, here was the conundrum, one I know that all of you share at your respective agencies—she actively abused methamphetamine and possessed a long history of abusing methamphetamine. Therefore, the etiology of her symptomology remained ambiguous. Was she presenting with a mixed manic-depressive state because of a more naturally occurring biochemical dysfunction in her neurology or was she experiencing them acutely from her drug abuse, chronically due to neurological damage from chronic use, or really, all of the above?

"She said that whenever she felt constrained and trapped like there was no hope, she would relapse and slam metham- phetamine. As a consequence, she would stay up for days at a time and engage in highly dangerous activities, such as unprotected casual sex, theft, and home invasion. She had two felonies on her record, one for armed robbery and one for assault, both drug-related.

"Moreover, while I was exploring her biopsychosocial history, she revealed that she came from problematic family relations. Her mother was an alcoholic; she was abusive towards the client when she was young. I'll spare you details. Her father was never in the scene; however, two of her mother's innumerable boyfriends actively sexually abused her: one for approximately six months when she was six years old, the other for about a year and a half when she was twelve. She stated that others made advances, but she resisted. By then she was in her teenage years. She willfully slept with one of her mother's boyfriends at sixteen, although this was still statutory rape. Unsurprisingly, many of these men, in addition to her mother, often emotionally abused her, verbally demeaned her, and struck her. Perhaps due to these circumstances, she began her methamphetamine abuse at the age of fourteen. Thus, although she didn't report symptoms completely consistent with posttraumatic stress, I am positive she at one point suffered from it—she experienced episodes of complicated and complex trauma—and this isn't even paying homage to her time on the street. After a series of horrible relationships with drug-addicted and abusive men, becoming alienated from almost every family member due to her unstable interpersonal relational skills, and a couple 5150's due to substance-related psychosis and suicidal ideation, she became homeless. In one session later on, she alluded to engaging in prostitution. She was probably raped more than once.

"Oh, yes, in terms of her medical history, the client reported no anomalies at birth; however, a frequency of intense ear infections at an early age, which resulted in hearing loss. She said she was Hep C positive but HIV negative. She had suffered two concussions in life—one from a mother's boyfriend when she was twelve, who also broke her arm and the other in her early twenties. Both were to the back of her head. Hypothyroidism also ran in her family. At the time of intake, she did not possess knowledge of her own susceptibility to its processes.

"So, we have her multifarious and complicated traumatic past, the beginning of a substance abuse problem with methamphetamine, and the onset of her first manic and depressive episodes in conjunction with physiological trauma and a potential thyroid disorder. We haven't even made mention of her Axis II features. Research shows that individuals, and more specifically women, with these historic features often present with personality dysfunction more or less in correlation with the fear and anxiety grouping and/or of the borderline and histrionic spectrum. This client presented with dependent features, histrionic hyper-sexuality."

My eyes landed on a female program director in her mid-thirties. She leaned forward, allowing her low-cut top to express itself all the more. She always dressed very sensually, at least in meetings; she always made sure that I could see the geography of her bosom. I hadn't meant to look her way as I used the word histrionic. When our eyes met, she had a fervent stoic cast. We exchanged a communication—perhaps she acknowledged my unspoken judgment—I'll never know—the moment was so fleeting. Tragic—since it is these moments that define relations—and yet they are so quick, so irreducible, never recognized, and therefore so inextricably free from definition. All conversation, all coordination becomes shackled in slavery to what imaginatively never was.

"…And attention seeking behavior, and impairments in her interpersonal skills reminiscent of borderline—although, of course, I make a purposeful utilization of the word 'features,' since I am unsure of their universal presence. As we all know, an unchecked substance abuse problem, and one especially in interlocution with an induced or naturally organic bipolar phenomenon, can present exactly the same way in social functioning—only once these two causative factors are contained and time passes, therapeutically, can these behaviors be more scientifically observed and diagnosed in this sphere."

"So how did she respond to treatment?" the navigator said supportively with the slightest trace of impatience.

"At first, she responded very well. I engaged her in individual sessions." For some reason, I turned red. "…Twice a week for the first month in order to build rapport and link her to other services at the agency. She met with her psychiatrist, Dr. Weisman, weekly for the first month, and then monthly, and she interacted with our case managers on a regular basis. The psychiatrist corroborated the ambiguities of her diagnosis, requested labs, and after he had satisfied himself with their readings on the client's liver health and her negative drug test, he prescribed an anti-convulsant in coordination with an anti-depressant. Of course, we also stabilized her living situation by placing her in transitional housing and our case managers helped her to obtain another driver's license, a primary care physician, and food resources. By the end of the first month, she reported that she felt less sad, less panicked, more hopeful, but absolutely restless. On the PHQ-9 scale, her depressive symptom quantification had diminished significantly."

I smiled gravely and stole a rest. A few attendants shifted in their seats as if they were uncomfortable. The navigator continued to patronize me, and in the literal and diplomatic sense of the word, and rather genteelly.

This was war. I would beat them with my meticulousness.

"Oh, yes. Her long-term goal was to improve her family relations, more specifically, her relationship with her children, by becoming more stable. To start the process, our short-term goals were to decrease her use of methamphetamine from four times a week to zero times a week, to increase her compliance with medication from four times a week to daily, since she had a history of ineffective outpatient treatment where she failed to remain evenly compliant with her psychotropic regimen, to increase her opportunity at acquiring stable and appropriate living arrangements, and to spend at least two hours a month on psychoeducation and parenting. The mid-range goal was work preparation or cosmetology school."

"And what did you run into during the treatment process?"

In past meetings, other representatives would chime in and add their affirmations or thoughts, or they would be unable to restrain themselves, much akin to adult children, and disclose their equivocal experience. However, here, there was no chirping. An entire long table shifted in focus between the navigator and myself.

"Well—that is a good question, once again, excuse me for my long-windedness—this is where I was going—the client, although she was responsive in the beginning stage of treatment, started to exhibit a cyclical behavioral process. She tested clean for about a month and a half, the bruises on her arms healed, you know, from slamming, and she had enrolled in community college to take just a couple classes to start attaining her general education."

"Oh, dear, so soon? Did that overwhelm her? That's so soon, she hadn't recovered yet it sounds like."

"Yeah," the woman with the low-cut shirt nodded astutely in concord. Her face appeared terribly objective. "Usually, in our program, when the client has a bad substance abuse problem, we wait until they complete a program."

"Here was our clinical decision." I awaited their complete attention. "This client had a number of strengths that, in the end, were problematically mediated by her deficits. She was articulate. She was attractive." I thanked God that I didn't flinch. "She had the ability to appear well put together—and she knew this. Combine these features with a lingering hypomania that was defiant of her medication regimen, and what you have is a driven, restless, uncontainable individual with impaired judgment and insight. At first, she was helping with her youngest child, but even then, she had too much free time. With her disposition, too much free time was dangerous and inevitably disastrous. She rejected inpatient substance abuse treatment since she had done them before and was very impatient with her process. So we enrolled her in outpatient and offered more extensive therapy and rehabilitative attention, but she became obsessed with attending school. Thus, as per the clinical axiom states, we started where she was—we helped her enroll and encouraged her to reflect and accept classes that she could navigate, such as remedial English, math, and a gym class."

The women both nodded as if to surrender their former challenge to my credibility. All around, the other program directors and representatives joined in, crossing eyes somberly and knowledgeably, some with a meek pinch to their chin or cheek, others with a light shrug, as if to highlight the 'what can you do?' powerlessness so intrinsic to patron sainthood.

"She relapsed," I said heavily, lowering my head to highlight the weight of my message, "...she felt isolated at school, made one friend but then turned him away after engaging in casual sex with him and crossing boundaries of emotional intimacy entirely too soon and impetuously. The father of her youngest son had started to nag her to fulfill her basic responsibilities as a mother, which she started to neglect. Her symptoms aggravated with her tension and stress levels; she ended up slamming methamphetamine again and decompensated quickly. We intervened hurriedly and engaged her in intensive services. She persistently refrained from inpatient substance abuse treatment but retained her outpatient. I facilitated a few family therapy sessions to delineate the family system while offering psychoeducation. Again, she improved, became medication compliant, and ceased her abuse of drugs. Our treatment team realized her cycle when approximately a month and a half later, she again decompensated after relapse, which, according to her, was triggered by hopelessness, but which we clinically also made note seemed to have a cause in the accumulation of stress in relation to her underlying biochemical dysfunction, her propensity for mania, which in turn was complicated by her subaltern relational dysfunctions to the extent that medication could not completely curb her symptoms."

"Harm reduction?" Another attendee disingenuously upturned her palms with little faith.

"Yes. She wasn't responsive."

"She sounded like she needed a different treatment approach. Perhaps ACT would have been more suitable for her.

Your agency operates on the more traditional field-capable therapy plus case management linkage approach, right?"

She came from a well reputable agency with innumerable programs that utilized ACT. I understood her suggestion as an underhanded promotion of her agency.

"Yes—and perhaps. Who am I to say?"

"She was 5150, correct?" the navigator said. She seemed outwardly impatient now.

I looked around the room—there was a new tension and boredom. The Inquisition was faltering. Where there wasn't blood, the hyenas grew tired.

"Well—"

"Feel free to give us only what you feel is important," the navigator said, interrupting me decisively with a film of gentility, "your case presentation has been excellent—very thorough—but unfortunately, we have other things to discuss as well."

"Ok. Yes. She was 5150. After her last relapse, she threw her medication away, and we lost contact. I searched for her four times and, of course, documented my efforts. In the midst of her mania and substance-induced psychosis, she attempted to take her life after returning home to see her son, who I suppose was being watched by her mother while she was out partying. I could never get the facts straight since her mother's report seemed guilty and dubious. At any rate, child services became involved, and her son was removed from her physical custody and placed with the father. After this occurrence, our team facilitated an intervention to reincorporate her into regular contact with the agency and remap an updated and more appropriate treatment plan. She agreed to inpatient and at that moment did not meet LPS criteria so we could not hospitalize her. After this, she disappeared. We similarly have documentation that we searched for her."

There was silence in the room. I lowered my head in wait. Attention fell upon the navigator. Her expression was flat—but flat in the manner of a lordship worn by the ebbs and flows of innumerable bitter judgments over years of penal servitude— branch or sword, it mattered not: in this game, peace was vile and an unproductive battle, reprehensible. After a split second, however, she offered a shadow of a somber smile. She had an expression that seemed conceding and displeased at once, although suitably satiated—and thankfully—I guess I had succeeded in my apologia. Mr. Giuseppe would be pleased.

"Thank you," she said. "Now, how's Napoleon?" She finished, whimsical and unruly. Everyone laughed—including me. We moved on. Irene Garcia no longer existed here, and she never did.

From there we discussed logistics and niceties.

II

I got back to the office around 12:30 pm. I had to report back to Mr. Giuseppe, write approximately eight clinical notes, telephone about five clients and schedule psychiatric appointments for them, coordinate the scheduling of case management services for an additional three with the agency driver and a case manager, become caught up in whatever else coerced my attention, and be out of the office by 2:30 pm at the latest so that I could follow up with Napoleon and Lenore at their residences.

Mr. Giuseppe and Paul were indeed pleased with my performance with DMH. Giuseppe didn't congratulate me, however, but he certainly congratulated himself for training me. Paul asked a few overly technical questions in order to demonstrate his expertise. By the time we finished, it was 1:18 pm.

Haphazardly, in a whirl, I construed my notes. I utilized archetypes again and adjusted them to more or less fit within the tyranny of the closing moment. Only after I looked at the time after my final note did I realize I was hunched over, my shoulders and neck stiffened, my breaths shallow and quick: 2:05 pm.

Phone calls. It all blurred together. "Hey, how are you?" I said.

"Good."

"That's good to hear. Would you like to see Dr. Weisman?"

"Yeah, I'm out of medications. I haven't had any for a week."

The voice was whiny. Somewhere, a hundred miles away, a cockroach squeaked into a phone.

"You missed your last two or three appointments."

"I was sick, and then I never got a call, and I don't think I missed that many, no, I only missed one, and that was because—"

"Alright, how about this Thursday?"

"Fine."

"Can you get here by bus?"

I heard a disgruntled noise.

"I need transportation."

"Ok."

I repeated the process. I realized I had almost forgotten another client of mine. 2:35 pm.

By the time I finished all my other tasks, which included having to sit with a random community walk-in with mild anxiety who nevertheless thought his life was over—I had to conduct a risk assessment and perform a crisis intervention—and moreover, which included all the unspoken social pandering I always had to do between professional tasks in order to keep the political peace of an agency where nerves were eternally and irreparably untwined—the afternoon already threatened to abandon me to the cold care of the evening.

3:50 pm. I said my goodbyes and made my exit. I felt oppressed by the fact that I still had to stop, as hastily as it would be, for the purposes of sustenance.

III

"Iosef, come in," a young woman said, waiting awkwardly at the door.

It was almost five o'clock, and I was approximately an hour and a half behind schedule.

My world felt disjointed, slow, and disproportioned. I stepped in, realizing that as I turned to greet this woman I was close enough to kiss her.

"Hello, Cassandra," I said.

"Have a seat," she said, directing me in. She lowered her voice and generally appeared both conspiratorial and excited. "He's doing so much better. He's been taking his medications. I," she said, taking care to emphasize her role, "have been making sure of it. He's stopped his freak outs and hasn't been...well, you know."

"That's great. How's your mother doing about it?"

"She's way happier too, but of course on edge as always." Her voice dropped. "She's such a pain in the ass. Want me to go get her?"

"No, no—I think...I think...yes, I think I should speak with Napoleon first, and then meet with you and your mother. That seems best."

She ran off. Her tone was rough and bossy as she called her brother's name. She did not return, but I heard the rustling of her brother from the farthest corners of the house.

As I waited, I appreciated a new hole in the white plaster of the living room wall that was a little larger than the size of a fist. I remembered the gun again. To counter, I tried to appreciate the dimness of the living room, which was sparse in property yet very regimented in order to convey a wealth from nothing. A pristine flat screen television stared at me, however, which I thought was strange. It must have been a recent purchase, but it collided with an antiquated antennae radio and a dungy fibrous sofa. Odd static and indistinguishable murmurs in Spanish emerged from the former.

"Uhm, hello," an almost unrecognizable voice said. It was tremulous.

Napoleon edged out from the hallway. Wearing a faded white t-shirt and black jean shorts an inch shy of his knees, he shuffled over sheepishly.

"Hey Napoleon," I said. "Please, take a seat, be comfortable."

"Uh, yes…yes…I am more comfortable here, yes…"

"Ok," I smiled. "Catch me up."

"…I-…I, uh… you know…just been here…doing what I…I've been, just in my room, yes, yes…you know…drawing a lot."

"Oh, that's great, you've been making good use of the art stuff I brought you?"

"Yes."

"Can I see some of your work?"

"…Well, uh…yes…I guess so…yes."

He did not move, though. He simply stared at the floor. After some time, he finally mustered the courage to break away. In jerky, hesitant motions, as his legs started to pull him towards the hallway, but in a disorganized fashion, his torso and especially his neck would twist back as if magnetically drawn to my location.

"Here," he said after scurrying back.

He sat down far beside me on the sofa and plopped down a sketchpad stained by coffee and what I think was semen.

"I-…I cannot say that these are good…" He looked preoccupied. "…Good representations, yes, of my art. I have been... I have been feeling very depressed and anxious. I do not like my medication. My thoughts are not at...at...at their former degree of clarity."

A sharp movement distracted me; his mother nimbly dashed between rooms in the background. I saw his sister peek out too.

"Wow," I said. "These are very interesting."

I saw shades, scribbles, nothing.

"Yes, they represent my great laboring..."

"Tell you what, instead of me paging through and paying only superficial attention, direct me to one that you would like me to see."

"This one."

He flipped to a dirty scramble of pencil shadings loosely depicting what appeared to be a disfigured humanoid strung up on an inverted cross—however, the man, with asymmetrical boogeyman eyes, had his legs spread widely and femininely. His hands were restrained behind the sword end.

"What's that say?"

There was script below the image. As far as I could tell, it was not an actual language.

"Uh, yes, it is a language you wouldn't understand," he paused. "It is an old language...but it is before...older...I became aware of it during my great purification...In Dolortictus Sonest Lovictus Salvator..." He spoke with an anxious pedantic flare. "...Roughly 'In Pain/Hurt/Condemnation there Are/Is/He/They Bring Labor/Love/Convicting He/Salvation/Purification/Destruction,'" he stopped. "No, no." His lips moved with an almost inaudible sound as he stared into space. "It's nothing," he said.

"No, no—go on, please," I said.

I realized he wasn't speaking to me and flinched.

"You said you do not like your medication?"

"No, it gives me anxiety."

"Which?"

"I like the Benadryl. It helps me sleep, but I don't like the Latuda. I am not going to take it."

"Napoleon. Your anxiety isn't a result of your medications. You've told me before that you have anxiety anyway. Remember, you said the same thing about Zyprexa so we switched you. The Latuda is important because it keeps your symptoms down—you know, the ones that have gotten you into trouble in the past. It helps with the uncomfortable feelings with your thoughts."

"I will not take it."

"Remember what Dr. Weisman said? —Your thinking is too fast to communicate your messag—"

"You will be raped by my light, understand? —I am your Lord, and I will not be spoken to in such a manner, no, you will listen to me, and you will be tortured by a thousand years of my minions—you," he raised two fingers, "you have just lost seven years of sleep."

Cassandra and her mother scampered out.

"Shush," his mother said. She rambled in Spanish. The radio in the background melded into her words.

"No, no—Napoleon is right. I shouldn't have spoken with such authority. I only did so because I care, but I have to be wary and always make sure that I am conducting myself with the utmost respect for my clients." I turned to him. "Do you accept my apology?"

He leered.

The white noise took over. I faintly recognized the religious character of the Spanish.

"Yes." He stormed away, nearly shoving his sister into the wall of the walkway. His mother cursed at him. He punched a wall without turning and disappeared.

For the next twenty minutes, I sat there with Cassandra and her mother. I gave witness to their commiserations. Napoleon's mother cried and cried and lamented her wretched life, telling me the same story all over again as if it was the first time. She profusely apologized to me for his rudeness as if this was the worst part of it all.

"Is my fault, my fault," she said. Sprays of bloodied *palabras* poured onto me from the spurting arteries of the martyr. "Oh, yes, you don't really speak Spanish."

I was impressed by the luster of her still-cordial smile, which, while dull, nevertheless survived the grime of her tears with resplendor. She gestured to her daughter to translate as if it was the most important thing in the world.

"She was just saying that it is all her fault." Her jaw became tight, and she became unsteady. "You know, what I was telling you before. He, the both of us really, you know, growing up around here, were exposed to a lot."

Cassandra suddenly fixed her top so that it didn't belie her stomach. Her eyes softened in a manner that defied the rest of her face.

"He used to see his sister, too," her mother said thickly.

"I thought we weren't going to talk about this again. I told you this isn't my fault," she said. "You were *our* mother. What were *you* doing?"

"This isn't the fault of anyone. I can only imagine what you have all been through and in these times, it is very common for emotions to become very powerful and for people to need an answer. And it usually has to do with blame."

Cassandra's hands curled in her lap. Her legs trembled and her breaths were fierce. With diligence, I maintained my focus above her neckline. Per contra, her mother presented herself with a thick veneer of pride like a self-righteous pygmy.

Tiredness, draining and evil, became me. They stared at me in wait, as if I was a judge.

"This has been plenty for today. Let me review a few things and then we'll schedule my next visit."

"When is he going to get better?" Napoleon's mother said, demandingly.

Both Cassandra and I winced at her desperate ignorance.

"Let him talk," Cassandra said, snapping at her mother.

"He is not getting better. What is this therapy for? You're not doing anything. We need the help, give him more medicine."

"I can't do that—"

"Aren't you his doctor?"

Her accent miffed me. I stared at her odiously.

"God, why are you so stupid? Listen to him. For the thousandth time, he is not his psychiatrist. He is a social worker. A therapist. Get it? Medication has nothing to do with him."

Her mother winced. So did I. She then guffawed rapturously. Immediately after, though, in place of any fight, tears started to pour from her eyes and she started to wail and wail. After a few moments of the proper theatrics, she returned her attention to me, apologized profusely again, and in sanctimonious tones, and then waddled with dexterity out of the room. Cassandra's face was buried in her hands. When she recovered, I saw no trace of tears. She sighed, exasperated, and I did too.

We talked about maintaining Napoleon's medication compliance for a minute or so. The tone of it was standard and strange. For the following ten or fifteen minutes, we simply discussed life.

IV

By the time I made it to the Bar and Grille after my final visit, it was 7:23 pm. Although I was supposed to see Lenore, I had an emergency consultation with a new client in the downtown area. So I called Lenore, canceled, briefly explored her progress over the phone, prescribed more homework, rescheduled, and rushed over to this other client's apartment. She resided downtown where the zombies walked. Thankfully, her domicile wasn't far from the bar I was due to arrive at.

This woman suffered from some schizoaffective disorder. I disturbed her graffiti session on what I think was a urine stained notepad. The writing did not travel from left to right; it flowed in all directions with multifarious tangents. The dirtied page was a maelstrom of symbols. I remember the profound unsettling that I experienced while trying to decipher it for any theme whatsoever.

"What are you writing?" I said.

"...Huh...What? Nothing, I'm writing nothing, well, I'm writing everything, when I was twenty Danny took me to his friend's house. He was a sweet man, very kind, and was involved in a church that tried to help people. He had worked as a security guard before..."

She whipped back and forth across her cluttered, suffocated studio apartment, never pausing in her spewing of mercurial gibberish.

"Did you use any drugs? It's ok if you did, I just need to know."

She stopped for a split-second, ran her hands through the grossly disheveled gray hair, and feigned innocence.

"Why did you call the crisis line?"

"I didn't," she said.

She peered up at me with some strange manner of teasing distrust and turned to the side to conceal her conspiratorial jottings as she continued to haphazardly scrawl. For a second, she went slack with her head turned towards the window. She dropped her plastic pen and froze, catatonic.

"I'm sorry to disturb you, but I have a few questions I have to ask people after they've called our crisis line."

She didn't respond.

"Do you want to kill yourself? Hello?" I said. "Do you want to kill yourself?"

"What?"

"Do you want to kill yourself?" I said.

"Do you want to kill yourself?" she repeated.

"No, I don't," I said.

"No, I don't," she said.

She mirrored my body language too.

"Do you want to hurt, or kill, anyone else?"

She indicated negatively.

"Good! That's good news," I said, "but I must hear you say it. I'm sorry."

"I have to hear you say it. I'm sorry."

Memories of childhood games popped into my head as I strategized how to out maneuver her.

"...I have to hear you say it, I'm sorry...," she said again, more mocking.

"I used the word 'must,' by the way," I said.

After a few more rounds of this I gave up and merely sat and watched. Eventually, she asked if I had cigarettes.

"Yes, I do. Ok. Here, sign this. It's a contract that says that you aren't going to kill yourself or anyone else."

The woman signed diagonally in wild scribbles, keeping my pen.

"Good enough. Remember, call 911 if you want to kill yourself or anyone else."

After briefly lecturing her on why it was a bad idea to abuse the crisis line, I gave her a few cigarettes that I kept in my bag for these occasions, and hurried towards the stairs of her refurbished building, which was pockmarked by the homeless and insane.

I pulled out my cell phone in a gruff. It was Paul.

"Hello?" I said.

"Hey, how did it go?"

"She was fine. No LPS criteria. False alarm. Crazy old woman, she was just scribbling. Probably smoked some spice."

"Ok, good. I'll call DMH. We have to stop taking these cases."

"See you tomorrow," I said.

"See you then. Thanks for going out."

"No problem."

I didn't know why he had thanked me. I had to go out.

"Oh, finally, look who decided to join us?" Lucia said.

I collapsed into the seat across from her. Her expression was supercilious, so I ran my fingers down my face. It felt good to pull my eyelids down and groan.

"What happened?" she said. "Got held up again? What did I say? You need a different job."

"A new crazy old lady on our client list made a call to the crisis line. I had to respond. It's ok."

Borges stopped the waitress and placed an order for a round of Old Fashioned drinks. Usually, Lucia sat snuggled into his right arm as he held her but tonight she crossed her legs and pressed her back against the obnoxious vinyl of the booth pillow, away from him. She was smoking a cigarette aggressively in quick, rough drags. Borges' face looked lackluster; his charm managed to survive his puffy, half-closed eyes, but not with his signature bravado. For the first time, I noticed that crow's feet had also made a landing on his affect.

"So, did you hear that the Occupy protesters got evicted?" Borges said.

"Yeah," I said.

"Good, you can jump into our conversation then," he said.

He lit a cigarette and took an indulgent puff, afterward holding it up at a foppish angle.

"If you don't occupy the mind, you are occupying nothing. Discuss amongst yourselves."

Borges had taken his time to take a taste of his axiom. He had leaned in and gestured poignantly with the finish of each clause. The whole show reeked of having been carefully thought out and rehearsed. Lucia finished her cigarette and impatiently started a new one, starving for it, bothered. It was evident that she had already grown very tired of the conversation.

"What do you mean?" I said.

"Think about it. What were the occupiers doing? What is occupation? It is the physical..." He was going to use the word 'occupation' but became insecure. "...Taking of space, it is the extension of yourself, of a body, whatever its size or number, into time and space. But what makes this specific occupation of space different from any other? I am occupying space right now, at this bar," he said.

The waitress returned with our drinks. I didn't want one yet but I accepted it. His excitement humiliated me. All I could do was nod encouragingly. The young woman accepted some cash that we piled onto the table, smiled cutely with a facetious air, likely in contempt, having also heard Borges talk, and left without any further word.

"What's the difference?" he said, wiping his mouth.

I shrugged but feigned enthusiasm as I listened.

"The difference is the *spirit*." He motioned deeply with his cigarette. "It's the purpose, there is a word for that in Greek. And it is found here. In the mind. It's the ideology, the ideas, the rising hegemony of new ideas and culture that is so important. Without their growth, without their freedom, their liberation into the masses of people, the extension of self into space is nothing, it is commonplace. What was necessary was the occupation of minds, not grasses."

"God. So you read the book I gave you. You're saying nothing. What do you think they were trying to do?" Lucia snapped. "Also, do we *always* have to have these conversations? We have already talked about this for like an hour. There is more to life than intellectual circle jerks."

"Well, what else can we talk about? Reality TV? And Iosef wasn't here and I want him to talk about it too. Anyway, to your first insinuation, yes, and that is the tragedy, can't you see?... Their purpose was to voice their ideas, to change the discourse, nationally and internationally, by demanding attention through the occupation of public space—but there was a reversal—the means, the political placing or extension of the self, became the end. And beyond the most superficial understandings in the public, it didn't impact the consciousness of the public."

There was no deeper satisfaction for this man than to speak the word 'consciousness.'

"Well?" he said to me before smashing the butt of his smoke in the ashtray. While he waited, he glanced between us and took a coy sip of his whiskey. "Come on, what do you think, for real?"

To tell the truth, I despised myself at that moment. I felt the pinch of dread and nervousness, for I was tired and did not know if I could articulate myself quite as fluidly as him—and so often, the mere fluidity of speech and thought is for some reason mistaken for intelligence. Other things occupied my mind—I saw Anaïs; she was a hang on to a different man at the bar—and this also contributed an immeasurable quantity of anxiety to my being. But I also found myself jealous—and this greatly agitated and disappointed me.

My voice almost shook, so fatigued with it all. "How do *you* know?"

Lucia yipped.

"Yeah, that shut him up," she said.

"Oh, come on," he said. "It's entirely more easy to tear something down than to construct. What do you mean?"

"Well, although I am not saying that presence is the only requisite of knowledge, I know that you were not at the Occupy encampment. Thus, I can doubt your familiarity with the state of the protesters. Otherwise, you're speaking in grand sweeps…you're speaking, ultimately, to subjects such as mass alienation of combined movements of force and the forces of causality, but how could you measure this?" I shrugged. "You can't. And this makes your thesis disconnected and, although lofty and articulate, questionably valid and definitely unreliable."

"And your little motto is a god damn platitude," Lucia said.

I winced. Her serpentine tone, I feared, added even more of a venomous and altogether oppositional flavor to the both of our rebuttals. This I had not intended, although, I couldn't help but feel the same satisfaction she must have experienced in effect. It was nice to see something inflated and glamorous rendered into shreds and frowns.

"Alright. You guys win."

Borges' affect darkened. In a beat, though, he recovered and mustered a forced laugh. I joined in and then Lucia.

"Cheers!" Borges held up his glass.

After we all clinked our drinks, he finished his whiskey expediently. He nearly gagged but seemed to overcome his nausea. "One more!" And he left the booth.

V

Some time had passed. Borges was still at the bar, languishing as he waited for more of the barkeep's attention. He looked stoic. All the usual gods and goddesses feasted around him, but he paid no direct heed. Lucia and I exchanged a pursed and dry communication concerning the scene.

She leaned in, speaking in hushed, low volumes—at least for a bar. "I can't stand him sometimes. Seriously, he's so god damned narcissistic." She emulated his voice and poised herself quickly and sneakily to his likeness. "I'm so other-worldly and dashing." She lit another cigarette, took a puff, and exhaled gruffly. "We've been fighting."

I looked over and watched as he placed an order. Out of my peripherals, I saw that he became aware of my attention as I turned back to Lucia.

"Catch me up," I said.

"I don't know. I'm just getting too old for this. I'm going to be thirty soon. I need someone mature enough to feel comfortable...I need someone who isn't so obsessed with having fun and appearances...I don't know. Someone who isn't afraid and anxious about a genuine display of affection."

"Well, you're the one who finds the beauties. *A rey muerto, rey puesto.*"

"*Desgracia compartida, menos sentida,*" Lucia shot back. "What's going on with you?"

I automatically shifted. My conscientiousness of this forced even more discomfort, as per the usual. The look in her eye related that she was painfully aware of my neuroses—and again, this only inflamed the sore.

"You need to get over yourself," she said. "Get out of your head. You're always so mopey. I don't get you. Maybe you need therapy," she added diminutively.

"Stop," I said.

She snapped her fingers.

"Hey! Out here," she said. "You can be so social and fun, just start being like that, and say things spontaneously. You're too cognitive. I've seen you when you're in the zone and relaxed, so many girls want you."

I followed her glance to the bar. Now Borges was holding yet another new whiskey. He leaned on the bar lethargically.

His smile was fuzzy, droopy. He was speaking to Anaïs, who touched his chest laughingly. His drunken and smug half-smile made it obvious that he had just captured her with a joke. He looked over at us and waved. Anaïs and I made eye contact, and her expression contorted in surprise.

"See what kind of bullshit I have to deal with? Why does he think that's ok? Does he have absolutely no consideration for my feelings? I trust him, I know he's not going to do anything with her, but still, what the fuck? I'm right here, have some god damned consideration."

"You're too negative. So he's chatting at the bar and being a little flirty, so he's flamboyant and superficial—considering that this is the only type you bring around, I'd say that for whatever reason, that is what you love. But it comes with its consequences. *Donde hay humo, hay calor.*"

"*El pecado se paga con la muerte.*" Lucia smashed her fist on the table.

"*Hay! Stalina!*" I laughed.

Borges' eyes goggled. He swayed at the front of the booth. "*Hay! Descansa!*" He slurred with an accent barely thicker than mine.

Lucia glared at him and tugged him into the booth. He yelped. His drink splashed everywhere. I became completely overwhelmed, agitated, embarrassed, disorganized, and foolish in my behavior as I very quickly realized that the feminine laugh joining my own was not Lucia's, who was then occupied with the submitting of the pouty Borges, who ogled into her irascible scolding with his comically large eyes, but rather belonged to Anaïs, who was now lowering herself into the booth beside me.

"I brought Iosef a friend," Borges said.

Lucia became giddy, the anger having dissipated. Borges kissed her softly on the forehead. She collapsed into him. At that moment, something changed. I became affected, warm, and acutely aware of the body next to me.

"Hi there, movie star," Anaïs said.

She was gorgeous and I couldn't stop staring at the fullness of her dark hair, which coupled the tight violet of her dress. I smiled—and quite naturally—and I knew that once again, a spell had been lifted, and all my charisma returned. No longer was it suppressed, or in mutiny.

"Hi there," I said, and laughed.

The rest of the evening at the bar was enchanting, even for me. I cannot even remember the details. I am happy that I can't. I was drunk, and it was like I was a different person, a prince. That night, I captured Anaïs. I got her number and we actually ended up going off by ourselves. And 'all of a sudden,' how I detest that phrase, although it nevertheless fits so perfectly, I 'hadn't a care in the world.' These things I did remember.

How horrible, how typical, how cliché is love. A thought-less homunculus, I was, genuinely ecstatic for the first time in months, and because of something so trite.

VI

O melancholia, thank you for returning.

I couldn't sleep. The rumble in my person, which shook me with its relentless volume, was a quality of misery only possible after a paroxysm of joy and nervous excitement. When these sentiments receded, they left behind a cold desert. This type of happiness preceding sadness was indeed cruel—it was a selfish glutton that devoured the holiday feast with such havoc that it left the house in a state of naught.

What was I going to do?

How could I talk to her?

I was an alien. Could it be possible that a creature such as I could honestly and intimately connect with this sprite? What was her experience, upon what was her soul predicated, what constituted her spirit?

I have done nothing but work and writhe. Misery is a subject I can converse about well, but the subject was no adequate vessel for the typical exchange and dialogue.

I was a fool to privy such fantasies.

After glancing at the clock, I realized that it was 3:32 am and that I was supposed to arise in three or so hours. I had made it home at approximately 1:20 am but I had been unable to capture any restful sleep once the night's activities had concluded at approximately 2:02 am. Again and again, I came to the realization that even when I thought I had been sleeping, all I had really been doing was staring at the amorphous storms behind the shades of my eyes. I would open my eyes in a daze to test my reality and watch the uneven density and dexterity of the ghosts above me morph and shift like clouds into one and one.

I smelled the sour gust of alcohol permeating my breath, and hers.

I turned over, carefully, as not to disturb Anaïs. I had the fitful urge to run my hand through her locks and then down her chest. Tears almost came to my eyes. For reasons beyond me, I pondered upon that old tale, *The Rape of the Lock*, by Alexander Pope. Barely audible to myself, I sniggered in restrained breaths at my silliness. Some thought processes, some emotions, were just so absurd. I breathed in deeply. She smelled like midnight dew and apricots.

She took my hand and placed it on her breast. After groggily peering at me more noticeably from what I suppose had been her own secret espionage all along, she pressed more closely against me. Her countenance made me blush; it was both tender and coyly patronizing.

"Sorry," I whispered.

Her form was so warm. I curled around it as she nestled into my chest and never had I felt so anxiously comfortable.

She laughed, and its flavor was subtle and sweet. She kissed me.

And finally, I was able to achieve what men need to achieve in order to feel like men. Because before I could not. However, by then, it was much too late. My year had passed.

We both fell asleep.

When I awoke, headachy and vertiginous, full of reaction, Anaïs was gone.

CHAPTER NINE

I

December arrived into my life with welcome. Ergo, it would seem fitting to assume that this welcoming of mine was due to some similar state of being—that perhaps because I was depressed, the discomfort of the season granted me peace by extending the experience of my inner world onto others, or through the matching of my usual internal state with the outer world. However, I cannot say that this was the case. Per contra, I don't remember ever being happier than in this time period. Although December winds had often brought me misery, and indeed did remind me of anteceding tribulations, this solely served to engender my current contentment with a queer nostalgia and a sense of triumph.

I guess Anaïs was my girlfriend now. After she had disappeared from my bedroom that night—that dreadful occasion of awkward masculine dysfunction—I made the decision to call her back. I did so with reluctance and masochism. And perhaps even with sadism, for what I would be doing was forcing her hand to hit me. Neither Borges nor Lucia ever knew about my inability to maintain an erection on that evening, so the both of them interpreted my long, shameful face as boyish cowardice. They chided me, so I suppose I didn't exactly deliberate autonomously.

While I expected to be ignored, or for her to respond with an awkward and extraneous social formalism, Anaïs instead responded with flat indifference. "Hey, how are you?" I texted to her about five days later. My phone chimed immediately. "Good, you?" she said.

I asked her out to dinner; she accepted. I didn't know why. The dinner went horribly. It was the first time we interacted under the auspices of God's sobriety when we had barely interacted at all. The night was filled with typical chatter. We discussed the weather, December, how depressing it usually was, family drama, and what kind of music we liked and the such. Our discourse was not entirely dissimilar to high school. We also talked about work. By some macabre coincidence, Anaïs was a case manager at Mission Hospital, which had an acute psychiatric ward. I had been there three times, and I think I had even seen her. After learning this, I distinctly recalled talking with her over the phone possibly. "Small world," she said. She didn't remember me. Nonetheless, we shared in the moment. If I am correct, it was this exchange in time and space that salvaged any probability of us dating further. The night was full of firsts, and it was the first time I saw the timid second-guessing of her jawline, the downtrodden turn of her previous clumsy and date-like coquettishness, the lackluster dimming of her affect...honestly, it was when I came to the conclusion that this woman had been fucked too many times, by too many men, and that she was just as lost in the world as I, and just as imprisoned in the purgatory of the mental health clinic. Desperation and despair were the forces warranting me the opportunity. The wise often remarked that God provides.

We kissed again that night. Anaïs looked terrified; her lips trembled as if from indecision between spurts of pointless questions as we walked towards our cars. We got to hers first, and she shifted about listlessly, avoiding eye contact. I said goodbye. She said goodbye too. I stepped in disjointedly. She still looked away. I blushed—I said goodbye again, my intonation askew and limping. She giggled, said goodbye as well, for the second time, made scant eye contact, and intently stared down. I leaned toward her robustly, stopping in the fashion of a mill tool just shy of her cheek for a quick switch into caution and tenderness. She flinched. Only after my hesitant touch did she finally turn into my lips.

We talked about every other day after that and saw each other once during the week and once on weekends. After a month, we talked daily and stayed at each other's apartments. She lived across the city, so this was difficult. Never since my early adolescence had I felt so amiable and human, despite the rain.

Work was sufficiently tolerable as well. No one remembered Irene Garcia. Her file slept now in our vault, locked away like a sarcophagus in the mausoleum of retired records. My clientele list was down to approximately seventeen people now from twenty. Two clients had been discharged since our agency had found their living situations relatively stable and we had three or four more discharges planned. The county was not questioning our clinical arithmetic due to the fact, supposedly, that we were currently handling some of the toughest cases in the region and because we had just successfully defended ourselves during the aforementioned situation. I found these politics extremely disingenuous. The only way I can think to make this clear is by accessing the Nichomachean distinction between Knowledge and Practical Wisdom. Every experienced clinician understands one axiom: that he or she is a clinician precisely because certainty is incommensurable with the therapeutic process. The phenomena that we study and interface with are of the category of things 'not apt to be known.' All we can do is utilize our reason, our intuition, and our ethical disposition to calculate the most parsimonious and beneficial process and ends for our clients and ourselves. We do our utmost best to dress this practice in all the décor of Science, perhaps out of egoism and perhaps out of subservience to the political economy of our lordships. So, when one of us falls to the theater of scrutiny, when we all switch places and don the regalia of the Inquisition, one day suffering and next day whipping, we do so with Sisyphean projection.

A discussion of my clinical labors in total is beyond me, but I can make note of my favorite cases. All a therapist needs is to demonstrate his or her effectiveness in approximately a fourth of any clientele. These successes deflect attention from the paralyzed cases. Actually, more—by providing evidence that the clinician is capable, it indirectly nourishes the inference that the reason the other clients do not progress is because of some other variable, which very likely has to do, ironically, with the very disposition for which they're being treated.

Both Lenore and Napoleon had shown signs of improvement in regards to their treatment plans. Lenore entered the program homelessly ('Client and her children are homeless 7 days a week'), with a methamphetamine dependence ('Client abuses methamphetamines 4-5x's a week'), and an underlying Bipolar syndrome ('Client experiences mood instability 4-5x's a week'). After years of instability, passivity, and indifference, it was only after she had started working with me that her participation in treatment improved. For the first time, she completed her journal homework assignments 'for cognitive and behavioral reconstruction.' She attended her psychiatric appointments more regularly, had started an outpatient substance abuse treatment program, and attended group therapy. Now, she was living in her apartment seven days a week through the financial assistance of our agency and her social security income, reporting no methamphetamine abuse, and experiencing mood instability approximately two to three days a week. Because of this, the state allowed her to keep major custody of her kids. Both Dr. Weisman and Mr.

Giuseppe bragged about the case. Apparently, Lenore was a resounding success story—but this narrative had equivocal meanings. For Dr. Weisman, this success signified competency. For Mr. Giuseppe, it represented political cache.

Napoleon, although he commenced our program living with his mother, still resided there to her personal but not moral chagrin. Seven hundred dollar checks for rent assistance from our agency softened that cross, of course. Napoleon reported his psychosis, mood instability, and anxiety on a daily basis and his lack of attendance at his community college as his presenting problems, in addition to his acute psychiatric hospitalization every other month or so. Our treatment goals were quantified accordingly: one, Napoleon would reduce his experiencing of auditory hallucinations, delusional thinking, and mood disturbances to approximately one day a week, on average, through his compliance with psychotropic medication, he would reduce his instances of acute hospitalization to zero times a month, and he would increase his attendance of college courses from zero to three days a week by the end of the year. He had yet to re-enroll in classes; however, he reported psychotic symptoms and/or mood disturbances only three times a week now. Furthermore, he had not been hospitalized in the past month. Thereby, he was also touted as a 'miraculous' success representing not only the efficacy and prestige of our agency, since Napoleon had been a notorious case in the county due to his threats and florid psychosis, but also my prowess as a clinician.

Now, did I believe in any of this?

I did not. Clinical algebra is only mathematics in semblance. Beneath this surface lurks an ominous universe of intangibles. Down there, there is only contingency, doubt, and the experiencing of qualia. "I was molested. I am dirty. I am a sinner. Now, I must become God." Is this not the particular manifestation of our universal creed? —and yet, although we commodify it, although we write it down and articulate it verbally, although we 'validate' it when its meaning emerges in paroxysms from the mouths of Napoleon, it is both ephemeral and ubiquitous.

I cannot speak of this any further. Is this not 'Truth?' By acknowledging this, as abstract as my reason is, I touch upon the salts of the earth—I am grounded—and herein lies the etiology of tragedy—for it is precisely this grounding that gives rise to my akathisia—I then see the entropy—and my consciousness becomes a feedback loop—a redoubling and reverberating echo of an asymmetrical synthesis of wisdom and illusion hopelessly tangled and therefore inestimable.

CHAPTER TEN

I

Paul rushed into my office, paying no attention to Heidi or to myself. He collapsed a tall stack of papers onto the spare desk and started sorting them.

"Here, give me half," I said and sat down beside him. I had finished my notes.

Paul kept doing what he was doing, ignoring me.

"I'll handle it," I said, more prompting.

He nodded and pulled his hair back. He did that when he was stressed. I pointed out a hair that had gone awry. His expression took a break from its consternation to acknowledge me wryly. But just as quickly, his face became slack again and swallowed the life of his jest. He took a deep breath and walked out of the room.

"Poor thing," Heidi said, "we're doing too much. How are we supposed to prepare for these audits, complete discharges, and all the while doing 75 percent? And Paul, can you imagine? He has to approve our notes."

I nodded. Paul was still seeing clients so she was alluding to his extra work. At least he got extra pay, I thought. I still had to attend those extra meetings for free.

"What is Giuseppe doing?" she said. "Paul is doing so much."

"Well…" I said quickly. "You're right, it isn't right. I don't know what's going on here, honestly."

"I'm so stressed. I can't even keep up with my cases, and we're supposed to be doing intensive services. Our case managers aren't doing anything. I'm a therapist, I'm not supposed to be doing their job," she said.

"Same here. But you know, they're behind too, I think."

"Oh, shut up."

"What?"

"You're not behind. And I hate that new client I asked you about." She grimaced. "He's coming today, you know."

Paul briskly walked back into the office. "Ok. I'm ready." He pulled back his hair again and exhaled gruffly. "Man, this place is crazy. Hey, you need to call the navigator for this service area back, she's been blowing up our line, and I've had to speak with her twice."

I shrugged. "Ok."

He was impatient and pressured. "Dude, just do it."

"Ok sir, would you like me to do that now or after group?"

He pretended to become distracted with something on Heidi's desk. He placed his hands on his hips and looked pensive. Heidi bit the inside of her lips and actually looked sorry.

"I'll call right now," I said.

As I got up to use the phone, Jolie interrupted us.

"Paul, line two is Franco, he said you were supposed to meet him in an hour to buy him groceries? And line three is one of Heidi's I think. She's yelling and cussing on the phone. She's saying that she wants to speak to 'the manager.' Giuseppe is here, but I was told to redirect the call to you."

Paul acquiesced. They both disappeared.

Marian popped in a few seconds later. "Anyone seen Paul?" She was holding a file and looked very concerned.

"No, but I'm sure he's around," I said, trying to buy him time.

I continued to organize the papers. The phone lines were almost full, but new calls continued to pour into the office. Mr. Giuseppe peeked in, smiled, and waved. He had his shades on and his carryall bag was over his shoulder, which meant that he was on his way out for the day.

"Direct all calls to Paul. I have to go to a meeting."

He didn't wait for any response. He finished his goodbye and disappeared.

II

A young man, delicately ratty, leered sardonically amidst the circle of the group.

"What's this group even about? What are we supposed to learn?"

Everyone in the group looked first to Paul and then to me. Lenore deferred to me especially. Napoleon kept to himself. Paul nodded in reception to their gazes. He was leaning forward, towards the table, with his elbows on his knees and looked relatively relaxed. However, sitting close to him, I could see that he was like one of those Roman statues of a man lying in leisure—tranquil in semblance from afar, even magnanimous, but noticeably cold and brittle once one became close enough for detailed observation.

"Well, like I said," Paul continued, "we are here today to discuss the process of coping with mental health symptoms."

The young man slouched in his seat. His arrogance appeared to be permanent and the sincerity of his comfort was apparent. He scoffed almost inaudibly. "What does that even mean…"

Paul stared at him for one long second. "Actually, that's precisely what we're here to discuss. Perhaps you would like to share your view?"

"Share my view of what? What does 'coping' even mean, what are mental health symptoms? You're the educated man. Why don't you tell me?"

"I think you—"

"Perhaps," I interrupted Paul. "Perhaps we should make that a discussion. That's a good way to start. We've discussed the general definitions of both things as a group, that coping is akin to the, to the manner in which people deal or circumvent their symptoms in a positive matter, and symptoms being the experiences, sensations, thoughts, et cetera, that manifest— well, that people suffering from a mental health, challenge, yes, that's a good word, live through."

"What the hell does manifest mean?" an unruly older client, a male in ragtag and soiled clothing, said with a pucker to his lips.

"Yeah," a young woman with heavy powder makeup said, exposing her rotted teeth. "What does that even mean?"

"Smoke break," a man in his thirties with a rough appearance, dressed in unwashed flannel clothing and a shaggy beanie shouted. He arose before any sanction could be given.

"Yeah, can we take a break to smoke?" another said.

"We haven't even started yet," Lenore interjected.

Paul remained quiet and stationary. I could see a faint tremor in his throat as if he wanted to speak, but he did not. We exchanged a glance, and I saw the lukewarm agitation in his expression.

"Guys, guys." I got up. "Come on, get it under control. We barely started. We can take a break in thirty minutes."

"Then we shouldn't start so late," the old man in the group said, his jaw shaking. "What kind of place is this. We put money in your pocket, and you think you know it all. You don't know shit. Waste of government money."

"Yeah," the flannelled man said as he shared a private moment with the powdered young woman. "We shouldn't start so late. I got things to do." It was apparent that he was merely trying to stoke the flames.

"Like herding cats…" Paul mumbled.

With more prompting from myself, everyone re-seated.

"Ok, we'll go around." I rested my gaze on the old man, who sat directly to my left at the roundtable. "Could you talk about what it is you experience and what you do to get through it?"

"What?" he said with volume begetting a yell.

"Your symptoms. And what you do to cope."

"Oh."

He appeared boggled.

"Well, I don't know. I guess I drink."

"You guess?" Lenore said.

"No cross-talk right now," Paul said.

"Yeah, when I feel like shit—and I feel like shit often—I sit back and have a drink to lighten my mood and forget things. What's wrong with that?"

"How often do you feel like that?" I said.

"Every day. I guess I feel bad whenever I want to drink. He-he."

Everyone sniggered.

The young woman raised her hand. "You know, more seriously," her voice was squeaky and her body language indeterminate, "I can identify with that. I feel like shit all the time, too." She looked at Paul and then crossed over to me. "You wanted to know what we go through, right? Well… I don't know, it's weird, I don't know how to explain it but, no matter where I go or what I do, I feel like…Well, I just don't feel comfortable."

117

"Like everyone is watching you?" a little chubby woman said, formerly silent save for the sounds of her tailing chuckles. She held her hands tightly in her lap and sat like a schoolgirl. She was in her fifties. "That's how I feel."

"Yeah, and like, I don't know, just weird things happen to me, like I'll hear things and trip out but that nobody else hears, and stuff like that. And like yeah, I'll trip, but others won't, then they think I'm weird or something."

"That happens to me too, but I thought it was just the booze. But then again," the old man became ever so pensive as a thousand tiny rusty gears churned in the recluses of his cranium, "when I'm not drinking—I don't even know if I'm in reality or fantasy."

Paul and I exchanged glances. The other group members remained either silent or withdrawn. Much of Paul's tension seemed to have melted off. I nodded subtly in support.

"Before we move on, we should allow others to speak who have not had a chance," Paul said. After making brief eye contact with Napoleon, who hid in the corner of the room just outside the circle, his demeanor and voice became entirely softer all the more. "How about you? Do you have anything you would like to share?"

Everyone turned to take crisp note of the Emperor, who had only recently retired. Wilson glared at him. Lenore became soft, almost motherly, and offered support in her expression. The young woman peered at him with hesitation, looking away often. The man with the beanie too became awkward; he smirked, but it didn't appear sarcastic—it seemed more nervous and out of place. Napoleon, who affected all strangers with his new litany of self-inflicted scars and his defensive, shifty, and wide eyes, practically shriveled into a coil.

"Don't make him talk," the old man said, flushed red with anger. "That just isn't right. Remember, we only participate in group if we want to."

The young woman turned to snap at the crotchety alcoholic. "No one is *making* anyone do anything."

Lenore sighed. "Guys, just stop. This shit gets old. We all know the rules. We never get anywhere."

"Ok, ok," I held out my arms.

Napoleon became aggressive. His hands, lined with the testimonies of his torture and purification, trembled into fists.

"Let's move on," Paul said.

"Let us all remember that here at group, well, yeah, here at group, it is about the opportunity to share and the opportunity to listen. What's good about it," the servility of my voice overpowered my nervousness, "…is that we can have access to others' experiences who wish to share and therefore understand ourselves better—and, you know, it's helpful to hear that others go through similar things. But no one has to share. It is voluntary."

Paul nodded.

Everyone in the room, perhaps feeling an apex of the tension, looked away and returned to only peripherally observing the Emperor. No longer the center of attention so openly, Napoleon unfurled his hands, although he still appeared defensive. He was now staring at a half-circular smudge on the white plaster of the wall, in silence, acutely aware of our presence, but nevertheless in deep and inaudible conversation with an invisible mouth on the wall. He sat there in vigilant interlocution, his attention nonetheless unfailing in its similar peripheral study of his enemies.

"Would anyone else like to share? Wilson?" Paul said.

Wilson redoubled his pompous demeanor. "Nope."

I handed out brochures on coping and began to review it. Once people had resettled, the conversation became lively again—but also only after Paul had mentioned the need to move on, recalling content from the last week's group session, which centered around drug use. Only then did the clients find an interest in discussing their experiences, but with a little bit too much excitement and nostalgia. Methamphetamine, cocaine, alcohol, and heroin all had their moments of mal-deference. "I started doing meth when I was fifteen," Lenore said, "...after that, it was over. You know, I got myself into situations. Now, I have some good days, a lot of good days thanks to this place, but I still have a lot of bad days. I haven't used in a long time, it has gotten better, but when I wake up, most days, I just want to stay in bed. I get that thought and I feel so guilty, you know?"

"Yeah," the beanie man said. "I've been clean for a few months...but it's like, I have these pains in my knees, and it's hard for me to move around." His eyes were searching and cocked. "I get really frustrated and in the past, it's just, I need it to move around now it's like. Jim, my friend, was going to give me that job...just been about, ready to go to school..."

"How about you?" the old man with the ruddy face said to Wilson, rough. "You don't talk. This is group. They wanted you to talk. You need to talk."

Wilson didn't respond. I went to speak, to remind the old man about the voluntariness of sharing I had just mentioned not too long before, and which he had even momentarily defended, but Paul stopped me.

"Well? You going to talk? It's about sharing your secrets, getting it out, and talking about your feelings, son."

"Why?" he said after taking a moment to puff up his answer with his version of profundity.

"What you mean why? I just told you."

Wilson shifted. The slightest tint of maroon washed over his cheeks. He started to play with the locks of his hair, looking more and more excruciatingly uncomfortable. Everyone chuckled.

120

"I understand. I've been there," the young woman squeaked, "it's hard to share, but eventually you have too, that's what group is for. You'll feel better."

"Why should I share anything, or talk about anything, when they don't know anything? They're just about control."

"All they have is their schooling and schooling ain't shit," the old man said.

"That's not true," Lenore said. "They do know stuff, maybe not everything, but they know enough to help us. And that's not the point. Group is about learning from each other because together we have way more experience, and I don't know, coping stuff. And don't tell me you want me to define that word. You seem smart, and I say that with respect. I think you know it."

"Could you clarify the control part of your statement? It would help us understand and perhaps we could learn," I said.

"Just what I said, you're here to control our conversation. You're the 'therapists,' you're here to facilitate man, and what do you think that means?"

The man wearing the beanie scoffed. "No disrespect too, but I think you need to think about what you're saying. You're here at group. If you didn't want to be 'controlled,' or at least influenced, which help is a form of, you know, yeah, then." He trailed off.

Wilson became peevish.

"They don't understand anything. Therefore how can they help me? Yeah, maybe they know some things, but no more than most people here." He looked at Lenore, agitated. "They are not scientists. And like this gentleman said," he motioned to the old man, "they rely on their books, but the books don't even know. And if they don't possess any real knowledge beyond common sense, then what are they doing? Influencing us with their opinion." He paused, having reclaimed his superciliousness, and by this, his comfort. He sat up and claimed his seat. "We're all here because we never had a fair and equal shot at succeeding in life, we live in an exploitative and oppressive society where the White Man controls everything. It's class, economic class. And as the one percent gets richer, we get poorer, and we have to find our own way to survive and feel good and cope," he used the word spitefully, "which leads us here, right? They don't want to give us good jobs, give us what we need socially, but they don't want us coming up on our own either, right?"

The clients started nodding.

"So here we are, in a program funded by the government, which is controlled by rich white men, a program intended to influence us to find happiness in our destitution and shitty situations and not to fight against what is expected of us. Right? This group isn't about injustice, it's about 'coping,' a keyword for learning to live in a pen, so yeah, I know the word. These men are tools, even if they don't realize it. And they know *nothing*."

"You know…" Paul said.

He didn't finish.

I felt the pressure mount in my chest.

All the clients fixated their attention onto us in expectation.

"For someone speaking a lot of sense, you sure avoided the question," said Lenore, much sharper now.

"Huh?" Wilson redoubled, becoming peeved again.

"Yeah, say it sister," the old man said as he started to clean his shirt off.

"If I was young, I would agree with you," Lenore continued, "hell, I used to say the exact same thing. I was alive at one time, *mijo*. You know what, screw it, in many senses you're right, the damn 'White Man' and the rich have been stealing everything for centuries. But when it comes down to it, they didn't make you do whatever it is you did to end up here. That's you. And you better deal with it. That's the toughest lesson, and no one wants you to learn it because then you'd have power. No white man forced me to do heroin, to drink, and to do meth, and all the shit I've done, God forgive me, so you just quiet up and think. Accept responsibility. They supply the needle, but you don't have to use it."

Wilson jumped up from his chair and threw it against the table. After it had only caused a slight rattle, he huffed and then threw it to the ground. It seemed sort of staged, his action, self-aware. Paul and I slowly arose from our seats. I extended my hands diplomatically.

"Everyone, take a breath—" I said.

"Boy, you better sit down," the old man barked.

"No cross-talk," Paul said. "Wilson? Perhaps you'd like to take a break?"

Wilson remained still. Without further word, he then found his way to the door with his head down. He threw it open and slammed it upon his exit. Paul pursued. I took over the group in his place.

Everyone at the table looked entertained, except for Napoleon, who had once again become perilous and tense before arising and scuttling out of the room as well.

"He's smart, he's just too young and proud," Lenore said. "I can understand what he's trying to say. I'm sorry if I made things worse. It's just…you have helped me so much, Iosef, and I see that you all work so hard. I'm tired of you guys being bullied."

The younger woman nodded in support. So did the beanie man and then the chubby one also joined in. Only the old man hesitated. "I guess you guys are alright," he said. "Still don't know shit though."

Instantly, I became embarrassed. "Ok, let's move on."

For the remainder of the time we discussed positive coping processes: routines, regular sleep patterns, healthy eating, journaling, other positive daily activities, exercise, deep breathing, meditation, and all the rest of these conversational topics in quite the cursory manner—it was the same thing we discussed every week—and every week, we discussed it almost, just almost as if it was new. And also just like every other group, one by one, the clients swore to commence these changes. The only person remaining who didn't continue to participate was Lenore. I saw her affect; it was guilty, harangued.

I concluded the group.

II

"You got quiet in group," I said.

We were in my office, alone, now.

Lenore shrugged. "So?"

"What's going on?"

"Nothing. Nothing, honey. I just got tired after all the bullshit. I'm sorry. I'm ok."

I waited.

"I saw your face."

"I'm ok. I swear. I was just trying to defend you." She gestured, frivolous. "It was dumb. I just got upset."

"I thank you for your thoughts, and for your intentions in group. But really, you should never feel like you need to defend me. This is about you. Let's do a check-in."

There was a thick pause. She looked away, agitated.

"Ok," I said, taking a breath. "Let's do this. Let's just review for a second. How's outpatient?"

"It's ok."

"Just ok?"

"It's the same shit, over and over again. What do you want me to say?"

"Like group?"

She ran her hand down her face. "No," she grumbled. "Not like group."

"Well, the Lenore I'm looking at is much more irritable and dysphoric than the one that I have seen in the recent past. I don't think it's just because of Wilson or group. What do you think is going on? Tell me more about outpatient, or whatever you want—"

"Life sucks, Iosef. I don't think you understand what it's like to be an addict."

"You're right. Help me to understand."

"Every day is the same, an unending stream of fuck-shit. I feel like crap. I feel better and then I feel worse. I'm a broken record myself. I'm going to be honest with you. I want to smoke meth. I want to smoke meth *bad*."

I winced.

"What's your program saying?"

"Don't?"

I laughed with her. Mine was awkward and hers was cutting.

"You know, the same stuff. 'Be mindful, avoid situations that make you think about it or make it worse, use your coping mechanisms,' the things that they always say. I can kind of identify with what that dumb kid said, and it bugs me. It *is* kind of insane! Hearing the same thing over and over." Her eyes lit up with dry humor. "Perhaps I need a better program?"

"Yeah, maybe."

For a few beats, we sat in silence.

"I want to tell you something about myself," I said. "My father went to a program once."

"Really?"

"Yeah, I never saw him again so I think it was a good one, too. Now, granted that you're still here, and care about your kids, and that you're such a good mom, I think you're doing fine in yours by comparison."

Lenore's eyes widened.

"I'm sorry. I shouldn't have said that."

"No, no." Her face softened. "It's ok. I needed humor, and that was sweet of you to say. Thank you for sharing with me."

Marian opened the door just then. She stopped and looked surprised. "Oh, sorry, I didn't know you were in session." Just as quickly, she left.

I turned red.

Lenore smiled.

"Thank you for your words in group," I said.

"You're welcome."

"Now, are you ok?"

"Yeah. I'm ok."

"When you came in, how much did you believe that you were going to relapse?"

"70 percent."

"How much do you believe that now?"

"5, 10 percent, maybe less."

"Ok, I'll take it. Remember, if you feel like you're about to make a bad decision, call the crisis line. One of us will answer."

I scrambled for some papers. "Here are some thought records to work on in addition to your journaling, if you find time. If you experience a bad thought, or feeling, work it out. But don't forget to put it in context. You arrived to us homeless, with an active drug problem, and with a mood that was all over the place. You were close to losing your kids. You've come a long way. Oh! Still taking your medications?"

"Yeah."

"Do you need to see the doc soon for a refill?"

"No, no—I should be fine for another two weeks."

"I'll pencil you in, anyway."

"Ok."

"Oh, how *are* your kids, anyway?"

"Good. They're good. Thanks for asking."

I waved away her thanks cordially.

We exchanged parting words and I showed her out. As we left the office, she looked much more content in disposition; she even looked relieved. But then something dark, even incredulous came into her eyes. I can only imagine that the very same look then came into mine.

Then, she was gone.

III

Heidi was busy with Wilson when I emerged. Apparently, after Paul had accompanied him outside, Heidi had been quick to take his place, probably because Wilson was her client. This freed up Paul to attend to Napoleon for me since I was with Lenore. Everyone looked miserable. Enervated.

I took a moment to appreciate the semblance of an exchange between Heidi and Wilson. Heidi patiently and calmly gestured with her hands as she spoke. However, she appeared harangued and condescending in her weariness. Wilson crossed his arms. I saw him talk in spurts. He'd lean into his words. Such violence, I thought. And then I walked away, not caring, or trying to convince myself not to care.

"Iosef," Jolie said.

She looked flustered.

"We got a call from Paul's client, the one he was allegedly supposed to see, Franco. He said it's an emergency, and he needs Paul now."

I shrugged and indicated Paul's general direction. She frowned and started off quickly.

"Wait," I said. "What line?"

"Four."

I briskly walked to my office.

"Hello? This is Iosef speaking."

"I said I needed Paul! Are you people stupid or something! Paul! Paul is my therapist!"

The masculine voice was scratchy and sounded deranged. There was a breathless rage to it. Immediately, I recalled the troubles Paul had been having with that particular client. "Sociopath," Paul had said in one meeting. He always threatened to kill himself if he didn't get what he wanted. He was the type of client that would not hesitate to complain to every supervisor at not only our agency but also DMH and the state government. In fact, he already had. He called on just about a weekly basis with his tantrums and threats, eventually always leaving messages at state offices all up and down the line.

"I am sorry, Paul is not available. I am Iosef, another FSP therapist, I believe I have met you?"

"What do you mean he's not available? He said he was going to visit me today, but then he switched it to tomorrow. I need groceries, what kind of program is this? You don't do anything for people. I need to eat, and you're supposed to take care of that for me. I'm going to fucking kill myself."

"Alright." I took a deep breath. "Let me do my best to understand the situation. Paul didn't show. You need groceries. And resultantly, you are experiencing suicidal thoughts? Remember, I am a mandated reporter, and I have to take that seriously."

"Wow, you're good at asking stupid questions. Yes, I'm going to hurt myself because of your stupid program. I don't need more drama in my life. You guys are supposed to *help* me."

"Ok, how do you plan on hurting yourself?" I started drumming my fingers on the table and observing the symmetry of my nails.

"What the fuck?"

I stayed silent.

"What kind of question is that?"

"Do you have a plan?"

"No."

"Have you ever tried before?"

"Yeah, I've been 5150'd!"

"For trying to kill yourself?"

"Technically."

"What does that mean?"

"You know, for doing too many drugs because I just can't handle my mental illness and decompositioning."

He had meant to say decompensating. He had also meant to say that he couldn't handle his crack-cocaine, which he liked very much—almost as much as trying to memorize our clinical language.

"Alright, well, from what you're telling me, you don't really want to kill yourself..." Paul walked in, alarmed and tired. I held up my hand. "...You're just feeling frustrated and are articulating, or expressing, this frustration. You don't have a plan, and you don't have a history of attempts."

He didn't answer.

"If you do experience those thoughts, or you do have the urge and a plan, I want you to call 911 immediately or contact us."

"I want my fucking groceries, man."

"...Because if you do begin to experience those thoughts and exhibit those behaviors, then we'd have to discuss a more appropriate pathway of treatment." I winked at Paul. He stared at me in suspense.

"What do you mean?"

"Well, if you're a threat to yourself, and you have a history of acute hospitalizations, then that demonstrates that you're gravely impaired and cannot make decisions for yourself responsibly. We'll have to work, in your interests, to have you publically conserved and transitioned to an institution for the mentally ill."

He didn't say anything. I didn't even hear his heavy panting.

"Sir? Alright, I'm calling 911 right now."

"Hum…no, I'm here. I'm alright. I feel better. Just tell Paul to call me. Thanks."

He hung up. Paul and I exchanged looks. Both of us burst into hysterics. Jolie peaked in and shared in the release. Paul's face was maroon and tussled. Tears welled up in his eyes, and he clutched his belly in a fit of wretched, inaudible gasps.

"…Iosef, oh my god, you're…"

He burst out again, uproarious, and squinted over at Jolie, who was smiling.

I wiped my eyes and took in a deep breath. "Least I can do."

And he nodded and smiled, almost reinvigorated. Heidi entered the office in an angry fugue and appeared mocked by our happiness. She collapsed into her chair. Jolie quickly exited, shaking away the last of her laughter. Paul and I both walked over to Heidi and started to prod.

"He's gone," she said, colorlessly. "So is Napoleon, by the way."

"Come on," Paul said. "It's late. None of us have even had lunch. Let's grab some food and get out of here. This place is too much."

III

The food at the restaurant was fatty and heavy but its cheapness compensated for the burdened flavor, which possessed an indulgent greasiness that I simply found wonderful. I had just finished the last of my chorizo. The coagulated cheddar melded with the pork sausage delightfully, and I found myself almost content as I took a sip of my beer.

Heidi poked me. "Why are you so mischievous?"

She pushed me again with childish assiduousness and generally seemed newly excited, like a young girl who had just been released from the gubernatorial oppressiveness of grounding from her parents. She wagged her leg back and forth. Paul watched her with interest. His hair was still a mash, but a new illumination breathed life into his face, despite the stubbornness of his weariness.

"What?" I said coyly.

"You do look like a different man, why are you so relaxed?" Paul said.

I was far from relaxed. I felt electric and cherry.

"Where you going after this?"

"Nowhere," I said brightly.

"Mhm," Heidi said, and she nudged Paul, who sat beside her. "Anaïs?"

I had started to flip through my phone. She had left me a message. "Maybe."

They exchanged a long glance. Heidi started to paddle the table in some form of camaraderie. When she finished, she wafted her fingers through Paul's hair. She started fixing it before finally messing it all up again. Paul acquiesced with a stupid expression and then meekly shoved her away.

I had an urge to ask about her boyfriend. However, I did not. Almost as if my thoughts had been heard, though, and quite loudly, Heidi rescinded her hand and pursed her lips, embarrassed by her freedom of action, which was so openly unladylike and quite immoral for open society. Paul looked at her sternly and squinted for just a brief moment as if to deride her.

"So," he turned to me, "how about all that bullshit today?" He shook his head and gulped his beer. "Mental health is insane." He continued to shift his head to and fro. "Only so much of this someone can take."

Heidi spiritedly interjected. "It's just the way that place is run. We need more organization. Any place needs organization. But especially when there's so much chaos from the clients, we cannot take it from above. But that's hard to do when you don't even feel supported. What was with those production quotas? I know I have been working hard. I bill for like seven hours a day at least, and I'm only at like 59 percent."

"Disheartening, isn't it?" Paul finally said.

"The case managers need to start assuming more responsibility. That way, we can focus more on our clients and know what the hell we're doing," she said.

Paul avoided eye contact. I assumed that he could also appreciate what I was appreciating.

"Wilson," I said.

She glared at me.

"What?"

"You're mad about Wilson." The words came out of my mouth freely and indifferently—really, apathetically. I shrugged.

"I'm mad about a lot of things."

"Like your shortcomings," I said.

Paul looked at me, alarmed. Heidi appeared up in arms.

"You're taking offense. But that's not how I mean it. They are not necessarily your shortcomings. They are just shortcomings. We all have them. It's sort of universal to our practice. Just is."

"Wilson—" She stopped due to a slight tremor. "Wilson," she said after achieving a greater degree of calmness, "is a malingerer. I don't have patience for him when so many others need services. I'm just overworked. I need time to think. I need quiet time. I need to go through the proper process, get to know my clients, assess them accurately, use validated and reliable psychometric measures. These clients need structure just as much as we do. We need to maintain a structured and focus intervention style, too much is demanded of us in too little time."

"Is Wilson really a malingerer?…Anyway, that's exactly what I'm talking about. That's what is ideal, that's what we need, but it's so formal, I don't know, do you understand what I mean? Your laments are mine too, it's just the way I see it, agency or not, those things are intrinsic to our profession as weaknesses I mean. I'm tired of it too."

I felt like crying. "I don't feel like I'm actually helping people, and I'm terrified of thinking it's because of me," I said.

Heidi said nothing but the anger slackened from her face. She looked away and exhaled brusquely. "Wilson is a malingerer."

"How can you know with certainty? We don't even understand our own psychology. How can we speak so authoritatively about his?"

"Let's change the subject, it's getting late anyway," Paul said.

My phone buzzed. It was Anaïs. "I need to get this."

I stepped out of the restaurant.

"Coming?"

Her voice was impatient.

"Yeah, of course," I said.

I peered back inside. Heidi looked solemn, and Paul leered awkwardly. He looked guilty. She looked furious and defeated. It almost looked like he was going to lean in and kiss her on the cheek. I hung up with Anaïs and walked back inside.

"I'm really sorry guys," I said. "I shouldn't have been so insensitive and flippant."

"It's ok," Heidi said, short.

Paul gave me a powerless look. "Let's go," he said, and they both arose from their seats and wandered out from the restaurant. I lagged behind them in vapid wonder, excruciatingly aware of the mechanical sweeps of my arms and legs.

IV

I arrived at the Bar and Grille with a familiar sensation that everything meant absolutely nothing, that all things existing breathed tubercular effluvium.

I bobbled over to the usual booth. As I clumsily floated, my panoptic vision unsteady on the surface of a river, I saw Anaïs on the same side of the booth as Lucia. She had her arm around her. Lucia was crying. I could tell by the rocking and the manner in which she covered her eyes. Notably, I saw no Borges.

"She broke up with Borges, we were calling you," Anaïs said—her voice was sharp and derisive. "Nice of you to show up."

"I had to work late," I said, feeling nothing yet, taking note of the fuzziness in my vision, "I'm sorry." I woke up a little. "What happened?"

"—We got into an...argument...that girl kept texting him and calling him...he just looked so guilty—I asked him, I meant to do so calmly, but I just got so mad...he said there was nothing...that I was acting disturbingly...I don't know what happened—I know he was cheating on me. Something was just so off."

I had the creeping suspicion that this man had done nothing wrong.

"Sweety," I said, trailing off.

Anaïs looked at me strangely. Lucia just kept on crying.

"When did this happen?"

"Just—just before—," she gasped to recover breaths, "—I came to the bar to meet Anaïs. He was supposed to come, but we ended up talking—and now we're broken up."

"Perhaps things can be mended, perhaps it was just meant to be."

My chest became increasingly pneumonic. I realized that I had said nothing.

I ordered us drinks, but we didn't really touch them. Anaïs and I listened to the feedback loop that was Lucia's honeycomb of despair and worldly forsakenness. Never again would she meet another man potentially so right and so perfect for her, she said. Her life was of no worth. She just couldn't shake her unbearable sadness. What had she done? She was a fool, etc., etc. She described her outburst as that of a psychotic bitch, the way she had argued with Borges. She would relent relentlessly, again tears would come, and the echoes of an evening's mortalities would circle.

"Look," I said. "If you love him, then you need to take a breath. You're too excitable. If you react this way every time, it is going to corrode the relationship. Just give it time. He'll reach out to you. If he doesn't, reach out to him."

"You're an asshole," she said.

"Isn't that what you have already said? I'm just tired of people making things so much worse when it is such an easy fix."

"You wouldn't understand, would you?"

"What's that supposed to mean?"

"You don't feel shit. You're in your own little world where only Iosef understands. There is no one else there."

Anaïs hugged her. "You'll be ok."

"I'm sorry," I said. "I'm sorry. I'm just tired. It will work out." I hesitated, feeling dejected. "I'll talk to him. I'll see if I can help. You love him. I'll fix it."

Lucia perked up. "Would you?"

"Yes."

Anaïs rubbed her head. "See? I told you he would help."

"Would you text him now?" Lucia said.

"I don't know if that's appropriate."

"What if he is with another girl after I blew up on him?" Her eyes welled up again.

"Sweety," Anaïs said.

And then it started all over again.

I felt strange because, with each circling, their fervor, our ritual, would remain in some state or law of equilibrium, but I couldn't help but feel the warmth with less force and attachment each round.

I had already been through too much that day.

By the time we left, Lucia had become more tranquil, but more so in the way of a sick person finding solace after the breaking of first of many fevers. She hugged Anaïs tightly and thanked her profusely. She called her a lovely friend. Lucia embraced me too, but it felt off when she did so like it was purely a formality, and for reasons well understood by us three.

That night at Anaïs' house, it was very quiet. We exchanged a few basic words and propositions of feeling, all of course concerning Lucia.

"Poor Lucia!"

"...yes, poor Lucia..."

"Can you believe Borges?"

"Yeah, the whole thing is just unacceptable."

"I hope she'll be ok."

"Yeah, I hope she'll be ok."

She looked at me with that same look that I recognized from earlier, one I couldn't completely interpret. "I love you," she said.

And I recited the catechism.

That night we also had sex. She did not moan, nor did I. There was little sound. Disquiet stirred in my abdomen as I ground on her, and I supposed this to be erotic.

V

Things were mostly humdrum for the next month. Borges reunited with Lucia. Truly, I cared not much anyway. Napoleon remained on the upswing, so that continued to be an accomplishment. We met at least once or twice a week to draw and color together. He loved to draw his eschatological fancies. I'd indulge him and compliment them, even if they were made of nothing but sticks, murder, and litter. "Yes, yes—that's a *brilliant* severed head, my friend." I'd never seen him so pleased, even daresay content, as when we had these exchanges. On his best days, we'd even get to talk about his shame, his shyness. Regardless, he was always in pain and his mood was a natural force like celestial rotation.

Lenore I didn't see as much. Something was different with her. Sessions became more rote, practiced, predictably doctrinaire. What zest she did have for therapy faded. Nonetheless, she continued. Anyway, a deluge of new high profile cases nearly inundated the clinic. My attention was forced elsewhere. It was for the best. Thus, our sessions were fewer, less revelatory, but at least her progress remained steady. I suspected relapses at times but her tests were always clean.

Things were finally turning against Mr. Giuseppe, too. People noticed his absenteeism, his deeds, his disrespect. His lack of supervision. The audit went terribly. If our bosses noticed anything, it was state penalties, even light ones. More and more, everyone gathered around Paul. Temporary shifts in power caused vicissitudes in popular alliances but eventually the political landscape settled plainly and without further spate. Mr. Giuseppe all but acquiesced. He conveniently used his vacation time, unable, I think, to face the very same scrutiny he once so freely dispensed. Heidi looked very apprehensive about the whole thing but for different reasons altogether.

Everything would change soon. Everything. I sensed it. I continued my philosophical work in private, and sometimes at lunch at work, almost thankful that I had lost out to Paul on that Tuesday long ago. Freedom from more responsibility supplied me with the time I needed for my ambitions, and I guess for Anaïs. For once I could visualize my future.

Never had I been so close to actually living. It felt febrile, but in a way that was much more restrained. I remained vacuous, though, adrift and apart from the warmth of other bodies.

So when my sleeplessness returned I thought nothing of it. I welcomed it.

CHAPTER ELEVEN

I

Que fait-on lorsque le soleil brille? On apprécie chaque instant de la vie de Dieu. February was a beautiful month. In ambiance, the airs, which tasted like raspberry gelato, fresh and delectably bittersweet and cool, which were the indubitably ripened leftovers from the cold disregard of mistress Winter, jubilated in a conspiracy with the sun and my joyful sentimentalities.

Sprightly, I occasioned my office building that morning with a bouquet of flowers and a box of dark chocolates. I snuck up behind Jolie.

"Hey!" She cried out in shock. "Iosef, you're bad!"

I graced her side, which was very full and voluptuous still. She had gained a little post new year weight, but it did not do her badly. Her tight spring dress invited my hand for the tickle as my eyes appreciated the not so subtle curve of her backside.

She caught me. I grinned, pulling my hand back.

"Happy Valentine's Day. These are for everyone."

She adopted a chiding and coquettish affectation and lightly shoved me. I set the flowers and candies aside before trotting away. If I wanted her I could have had her. This I knew as assuredly as a child knows his candy. I heard her voice as I escaped.

"What did you get Anaïs?"

I twinkled. "Nothing."

"You're going to be in trouble, Iosef," she yelled.

I waved to Marian on my way to my office. No longer was I rooming with Heidi. She remained in our old office room, which for me, wreaked like mothballs and altogether seemed suffocated. Now I possessed Paul's old office. Much more spacious, firstly—secondly, it was also all and one my own. It was nice to have an office just to myself. Finally, I could concentrate, I didn't have to battle the temptation of distraction via extraneous and meaningless external stimuli, e.g., conversation.

My office was closer to Dr. Weisman's, too, which was very convenient. If I so experienced the compulsion to socialize, I could pop by his dormitory and squabble about this or that psychiatric or philosophical problematic. I kept him abreast on my work. He delighted in my intellect. I delighted in his delight.

I placed my briefcase on the charcoaled turquoise-green carpeting beside my cushioned leather chair and dark cherry desk and turned just in time to catch Paul entering his office across the way. Of course, to entertain him, I performed a little morning dance and shimmied with my coffee cup in hand. He shook his head and laughed and then sipped at his coffee in mock tiredness, pretending to suffer the misery of a hangover.

Heidi passed by, preoccupied, stopping only briefly. "Meeting in ten minutes," she said, not waiting for me to say hello.

A new therapist hurried by my door in the same direction as Heidi. I forgot her name. She waved meekly as she rushed passed. Our other case manager, also new, did similarly. I wondered what was amiss but only for a single moment. In all truth, at that moment, I wasn't interested. Just as I wasn't interested in knowing any of them or the new interns. I collapsed into my chair mirthfully, smiled for no reason, and texted Lucia 'Happy Valentine's Day,' which I instructed her to pass onto Borges.

"Happy Valentine's Day," she responded, "I will." And a few moments later, "Borges says Happy Valentine's Day too. Did you text Anaïs?"

"Not yet," I said, and I ignored her response.

II

Everyone sat impatiently in the conference room. Idle chatter sounded off here and there in short little bursts as we awaited the arrival of Dr. Weisman. Paul sat at the head of the table on edge, his usual nerves only concealed by his occasional gestures of cordiality to hold people over.

This was only the second meeting that he had chaired as the new director of the FSP and FCCS programs since the sacking of Mr. Giuseppe. Although the circumstances of his prosecution were quite scandalous, there was no genuine acknowledgment of it, as the prophecy for it had already been well known. "Mr. Giuseppe is no longer with us," Paul had said, his voice relatively unsure of itself, "…and I have been instructed to tell you that you can no longer communicate with Seth during work hours, and that if you ever notice anything that you feel is not right, that does not befit the ethicalities of professionalism in any way, you are to inform me or our higher ups." I remember how he had paused, perhaps in self-observation that it was the first time that he had ever felt comfortable enough to use Mr. Giuseppe's first name.

Rumors had circulated a couple narratives about Mr. Giuseppe's exit. The disaster of an audit was clearly not explanation enough for his demise. In one rumor, Mr. Giuseppe had embezzled up to $20,000 dollars—a little at a time from the therapeutic programs' flex funds—by faking receipts of the drip-drab spending we had always done for our clients, such as for breakfast or lunch. In another, he had been sleeping with other employees. According to the imagination of one dire whisperer he had been sleeping with Jolie—but according to Jolie, he had been having sex with some unremarkable young girl that we had always seen in his office under the auspices of supervision. The girl wasn't with us long; she left her internship. Moreover, he never even supervised *us*. The fact that Giuseppe had hardly ever been present for his work, period, as previously stated, and had been conspicuously performing his duties in the most sloppy and perfunctory manner, lent abductive premises for any and all of these postulations.

Paul had played his cards well. Company executives arrived to coronate him before departing just as expediently. The fiefdom was his. Heidi and Paul discontinued sleeping together. This had been Paul's mandate although Heidi claimed that it was mutual. I knew the truth because Paul had told me, but I kept this to myself. By the end of the month office morale had improved overall, but oddly enough, inversely proportionate to Paul's personal well-being. The stress continued to wear on him, just as it did when he was lead therapist. Except now he shouldered even more amounts of it—and now he did so alone.

The Department of Mental Health, of course, was politely shielded from the uproar. "Mr. Giuseppe has resigned," I had to report at our last Thursday meeting. I feigned displeasure and sorrow. "That's too bad, etcetera, etcetera," was the gist of the responses. Notably, no one asked about details. Everyone became generally merry again, including me, without further thought. All too hastily, Mr. Giuseppe had gone the way of Irene Garcia. *C'est la vie mon enfant terrible.*

Finally, Dr. Weisman took his seat after strolling in, his expression unaffected by his lateness. "Good morning," he said smugly. He made no apologies. After rustling through his carry bag, he pulled out a piece of paper and the same black fountain pen that he always used when analyzing clients. He slammed the paper down to indicate that he was ready to begin.

Paul nodded. "Alright, we already have clients waiting in the lobby so we'll have to be efficient in our use of time."

"They can wait," Weisman said. "They're not going anywhere."

"Sure, sure," Paul said. "So, as you guys know, things are changing around here. Before, we would only meet for case presentations and discussions once in a while. In fact, other than our last one, we haven't met since I was last promoted. We weren't organized, and our work suffered for it. We have an excellent team here and we have a lot to learn from each other. So, let's review the cases we chose for the day. Remember, give a concise synopsis of the case first for our new people."

"It's also important because it's malpractice to do otherwise," Weisman said. "It was unconscionable what was going on here. We are running a small hospital, you know."

"You're absolutely right, Dr. Weisman," Paul said.

Heidi huffed. "It's a good point, but obviously, things are different now. Let's move on. I'll begin. Wilson," she stated bluntly. "Approximately twenty-five, Mexican-American, college student. Axis I, Psychotic NOS—"

"Malingerer," Weisman said.

Heidi flinched at the interruption, but then continued. "Reported symptoms include thought broadcasting, audio and visual hallucinations, non-bizarre delusions of persecution, paranoia, and grandiosity...but the client doesn't report these any longer..." She seemed to become distracted for a moment. "Anyway, he has Axis II features, narcissistic and features of anti-social. He reports no health problems and according to him, he's impaired in terms of primary and secondary support groups, and he has trouble in school. He was homeless when he arrived to us as a referral from a volunteer at the Occupy movement. He views himself as a revolutionary against a global conspiracy of the rich and powerful, which while we are not a part of, we indirectly serve through many mediated steps as some informal arm of the government."

Dr. Weisman chuckled again, dryly. "Malingerer. Next."

"Come on, Dr. Weisman. Let her finish. We're going to follow the rubric. You'll have your chance to comment. We respect your expertise but we have to keep it orderly," Paul said.

Weisman glanced at me subtly before looking back at Paul. "Ok."

"We've involved him in group," Heidi said. "He remains oppositional, but we've managed to subsidize a room for him since then, a sublet from another student, so now he isn't homeless. He says he is doing better in school. He isn't currently taking medication because, as the doctor has presented," she said emotionlessly, "he does not believe in the genuine nature of the symptoms. Anyway, I'm open to suggestions for interventions. He has been resistant to any real process."

Weisman raised his hand slightly and playfully, as if to ask for permission, but he didn't wait to be called on. "His entire presentation isn't congruent with his self-report. Visual hallucinations indicate an organic dysfunction." He tapped his head, bored with it all, and spoke flippantly and confidently. "But he doesn't hold up his presentation consistently. He has none of the other external features that come along with this. He says he's paranoid, that he fears the government, but he comes to me and asks me for help? Please. He's playing you. He isn't FSP. Discharge him."

"He would be homeless," Heidi said.

"He gets SSI. He's lucky I didn't evaluate him. He must have seen an inexperienced doctor."

Paul remained quiet. He was still red in the face and generally looked edgy and uncomfortable. True to form, he pulled his hair back. Dr. Weisman made note of this and became a little more restrained, if not even apologetic, like a father who had just played a little too rough with his oldest boy.

"Doctor?" I said. "Granted, I am also inexperienced." I pretended to fawn with humble rigor. "But just for my own information, my own education…"

"Sure, go ahead." As he spoke, he gestured to Paul in mild apology.

"Is it ever possible for someone who is of the psychotic spectrum to report these symptoms but have an atypical presentation? Do symptoms always correlate so cleanly with signs and behaviors? I can never resolve this for myself—like, what if they did experience visual hallucinations, and paranoia, but possessed enough grounding to retain some level of functioning or insight?"

"Mmm…" He frowned. "Of course, it's possible…but I would still say no…the behaviors must always correlate with the experience." He tapped his head again for effect. "If they're reporting paranoia then I'd expect to see some level or some minimal hesitation or distrust…but visual hallucinations? No. As I said, that indicates organic dysfunction and the physiognomic markers, which represent genetic and epigenetic markers correlating with them, would be observable. Usually, when someone reports visual hallucinations, there is an automatic process of rule out."

I nodded with a big, dumb smile. "Thank you."

"Well, Wilson does present with paranoia and distrust, he won't tell us anything," Heidi said, still lacking in any intonation, "but I am not sure, myself, anymore. I used to think the same as you, doctor, but now I don't know. I can't put my finger on it but he's giving me a really bad feeling. He just has this look in his eyes. Anyway, we'll continue supporting him as he goes to school and we'll review the case again before his next psychiatric appointment."

The doctor acknowledged this. He had become a little more settled and amicable, although he remained quite elevated in airs. He explained, as a disclaimer, that he would never actually hit the client with the malingering diagnosis for liability reasons, but he was fairly positive. Heidi again nodded and acknowledged the doctor. She quickly reviewed her other cases in a very cursory and simplistic fashion, which was very unlike her. She explicated her reasoning again and again in defense against the doctor's passive aggressive curiosities, which could have also just been his thoroughness. All the while, Paul did and said nothing, having apparently chosen to pick his new battles as chief. By the end of it, Heidi looked bereaved. I found it entertaining, these strange little power struggles.

The new interns went next, and then the new therapist. Everybody was warm and gentle with them, which created that much more of a sharp juxtaposition with Heidi's presentations and treatment.

By the time my turn arrived, I sat erect, confident, and I experienced no quakes. Instead, I felt the encouragement of an excited fervor, which informed me of my readiness to present. I had been preparing for this. Plus, it was one of those days that the fugue of everyday gloominess lifted its clouds, perhaps rescinding from the force of a recharged clarity. Everything truly seemed illuminated. This would not be like that one Tuesday, long ago. I cursed myself for being so squirrely, so timid, so insecure, immature, and incognizant of my purpose, role, and capabilities for so long. Friends and family always informed me of my potential, and while deep down I acknowledged their compliments, I rejected the very thought— for categories of such holiness could not rest peacefully upon my shoulders as descriptors. Now, let them be—that is what was said. Away with the merely prosaic.

"Napoleon Gigante will be first. We're all very familiar with his demographics so I will spare those details. I would like to offer an epistemological caveat first—typically, in our philosophy of science, in order to effectively and ethically treat a client, we must understand the relationship between the different variables at hand, at least the ones that are the most relevant. Then, we must isolate the variables that appear to be the most correlated and/or causal, although that word is indeed nebulous, and target those for treatment. Now that all that ruckus is over, and I am mostly caught up with documentation, I have spent a little more time reviewing and pontificating upon my cases." I looked around and saw blank faces. "Let me clarify quickly before moving on. The doctor here isolates certain variables neurochemically. Dysfunction in the flow and communication of neurotransmitters has been noted to correlate with certain mental health symptoms. Therefore, the doctor, after isolating the symptoms, makes the sound assumption, based upon a history of experience and research, that a medication he prescribed will work towards the relative amelioration of this dysfunction, thereby hopefully relieving the symptoms partially."

"Yes, that is more or less correct. You'd think there would be less conjecture, but not in this country," he said disgruntled. "We need more research."

"Our job, as therapists," I said pedantically, turning to the interns, "during our biopsychosocial assessment, is not to treat for every diffuse trauma or circumstance in their history, but to utilize their presenting problems as a bayou that keeps us safely tied to the client's intentionality as we explore deeper, from that point, to pick and isolate, over time, what is the most pivotal phenomenon to emphasize in therapy."

I took a deep breath; I realized I hadn't been breathing enough. I laughed. They laughed too, except for Heidi, who only chuckled lightly and distractedly, and Paul, who only smirked, quite similarly deflated or distracted. "Ok, to the point, sorry. Napoleon carries a diagnosis of Schizoaffective disorder, bipolar type."

Weisman raised his eyebrows at the word, 'carries.'

"He has a comorbid methamphetamine abuse problem and complains of severe anxiety. As many of you know, after abusing methamphetamine, he decompensated quite heavily and had to be 5150'd from here after presenting as a threat to others. It's pretty clear that stimulants are an eminent causal force in the exacerbation of his symptoms, and the nullification of his medication." I pursed my lips humorously. "Thus, the first thing we did was to work to decrease his abuse of methamphetamine. We succeeded here; he was afraid that without it, he would never *not* feel tired and depressed—and after a good length of psychoeducation for him and his family, he was convinced to stop using the drug under threats of being kicked out and after we told him that he could achieve higher energy levels through psychotropic medication and lifestyle changes. So far, so good."

I took a sip of my coffee and stole another breath. I didn't realize how fast I was talking before then. A moment passed and I composed myself.

"My first intervention was to appreciate the rapport building process. I have been visiting Napoleon's house regularly. Before, he treated me like a stranger, and I noticed that the anxiety, fear, and guardedness that arose from this seemed to trigger him into another prodromal state of mind. Now, he is comfortable with me, as are his sister and mother. I have yet to meet his other relatives. Anyway, I spend a lot of time asking him about his art. And it was that way that I found my way to what seemed relevant in his history. You see, he would draw some strange geometric figure, which turned out to be a series of crossed inverted crosses, shaded in all gothically. In synopsis, he told me that it was the good, inverted and corrupted, quite stereotypical, right? That's important to mark since stereotypical and/or magical thinking can be a symptom. Anyway, the multitude of them represented a totality, the process of the 'purification,' the amelioration of the inversion, and simultaneously and contradictorily, the absolute stasis of the phenomenon nevertheless. Philosophically, we could go down a rabbit hole, here—the relevant clinical point seemed to be this—he felt corrupted, he was trying to purify himself, saw this as an ongoing process, but nevertheless experienced hopelessness and a somewhat grave realization that his project was absurd, that stasis was inextricable regardless of any illusions of progress. This, in turn, led to his disclosure that he felt personally tainted with dirtiness and sin because he had been subjected to sexual abuse—he would only allude to this, however, and I had to utilize family reports as well—not only did he witness many crude acts, but a relation of their family, a male, was the perpetrator, which also explains his discomfort with male authority figures and therapists. This sense of self-odiousness and loss co-occurs with automatic negative thoughts, including sexual thoughts, about his family members. He is disgusted with himself. This, alongside numerous other complicated occurrences of trauma and marginalization, gives rise to a debilitating restlessness and anxiety, and a depression, which further impair his ability to function in social and occupational manners. What we had here was a reflexive process of degeneration. The client disclosed that he became absolutely isolated and miserable and started to feel his 'insanity,' his psychotic symptoms, developing at about the age of twenty. His discovery of methamphetamine ensured his psychotic break. So, we have a few variables from this. The etiology of his mood disorders is his sexual abuse and neglect,

149

compounded by the traumas of social, educational, and occupational impairments; the mitigating secondary variables arising from this complex are his sensations of sadness, hopelessness, and restless anxiety."

I beamed and quickly looked down, quick to restrain myself. I almost cried and had to conceal the formation of tears. Again, I remembered our last meeting of this nature, where I was ridiculed, humiliated, where I failed to present my capabilities. The urge passed. The floor was still mine.

"The interventions are never as complicated as the investigation, are they? In order to counter his mitigating variables, his symptoms, we've worked on positive daily activities, including coping mechanisms, and structured living as part of a task-centered plan towards more schooling. He is sleeping more regularly, going to bed and arising at more or less the same time, using his medications, and sketching or drawing as his method of circumventing his anxiety. The promise of a better future via schooling is the goal representing hope. We haven't discussed or processed his abuse, we aren't there yet, and maybe we never will be, but he is processing it through his art on his own and the fact that I am a male of relative authority, and am helping him, seems like it could be a positive thing. As per DMH, I guess this progress can be measured through two things. One, he has not been hospitalized, which is evidence of treatment efficacy since he has been hospitalized just about every month or two. And secondly, he is involved in more positive daily activities, as represented by his socialization with his family and his art."

I felt their eyes on me with much more gravity. Perhaps they were judging me. Perhaps they were in awe.

"It's not perfect...well, you know—the process...I am making the process seem entirely more pristine that it was."

Heidi was staring at me blankly now. Her and Paul exchanged odd glances. They knew me too well not to know that something was wrong. I was talking too much. Even I knew this.

"There are interesting dynamics in the home and between the sister and myself. No, no, no—not bad dynamics, not inappropriate dynamics, just interesting ones. I have to say her transference, well, I guess, yes, transference applies, and my countertransference, well, I'm just getting off track now."

I started to sweat. I avoided looking at anyone in the room.

"What are your plans?" Paul said. "I appreciate all your detail, but you do know that we already know pretty much everything about Napoleon, right? I know some staff here doesn't but we can keep the detail to a minimum."

I felt a kick. There was a phenomenal shift in my head. Everything moved to the right, although nothing moved.

"Oh, sorry, excuse me. I'm sorry. I'm just excited that we're doing these things, now. I thought I'd be thorough." I realized I was still sweating. I also realized just how fast I had been talking again. I feigned a cough and cleared my throat. I stared down at the carpet as I did so. I saw fuzziness. I focused again in that manner that is without focus. I saw the blackness moving in the conference room in the broad of daylight. Never before had I seen it while things were so bright.

"Where was I?"

"Your plans," Paul said.

"To continue with cognitive-developmental therapy," I said. My voice stammered, pressured. "He has stabilized, but really, we are only really beginning to map out his cognitions and his developmental stunts—I think the actual therapy can begin now. I'll continue to meet with him at least once or twice a week, check in, draw with him, and explore his belief systems and plans."

It was hard for me to pay attention to what I was saying now. Something else entirely, a homunculus, a familiar thing, now commandeered the functioning of my articulation as 'I' searched and observed the plethora of diffuse and dispersed phenomena of my internal state. Who was 'I'? How could I know this when the concept of 'I' was so heterologous?

"He's stable?"

Paul asked this skeptically. The doctor continued to look at me with displacement, difference, I don't know.

Information processing was automatic, and by automatic, I mean that it was done without my accord—their looks, their words, the meanings hanging loosely from them like fat and sloppy fruits half-picked, rotten, and burdening their branches, the meanings of my own, of my 'I,' the non-'I', the puppeteer of my meta-'I,' and this went on forever, all of it merely was, it all merely happened.

"Yes, he's stable as relative to before—and here, stability could be defined as a consistent repetition of his ADLs, the taking of his medication, the absence of LPS criteria, the diminishing of the severity of his symptoms, and as I said, the absence of new outbursts and hospitalizations."

What I said was redundant. I became terribly aware and obsessed. I did not choose to say those things. The words just came, but from where? Was my cortex alive? What ghost within that mush spun such nonsense, what basis did it have, what evidence? I wasn't even being concrete. What was the archaeology of these concepts…I did not create them…they came not from Napoleon…and these thoughts of mine, these were the 'I' or the 'meta-I'? If I needed to delineate the categories, how could I?

"…Of course…"

I was still talking. My face smiled. So beautifully, too, this man was so charming again. Despite the noise, the intonation of my voice seemed masterly in its erudite pronunciation and emphasis, and daunting in its rapidity.

"…And our goal is to finish helping him get SSI. We will also commence this process now that he is stable and grounded. And once he gets this, we can begin the discharge process, as, theoretically, he would then have the means for his own sustenance, rendering him ineligible for FSP. I know we keep people with SSI but perhaps our ability to help him will have been expired, so it would be best to move him on."

'I' was everywhere. After appreciating the swiftness of the black ash at my feet, I swallowed and inhaled deeply, exhaling with another cough as to cover up the mechanical awkwardness of my switch into manual control. I heard Paul say thank you. The doctor nodded. Heidi joined into the general consensus of bobbles. But I knew what they were doing. They were distracting. They were capricious, suspicious. It was all a show. They didn't understand. I didn't understand.

I talked for another fifteen minutes about Lenore's progress too. By then I felt like it was finally myself talking, but only thinly. I told them I suspected relapse and they nodded. "I'll check in with her soon." Again, I felt my face light on fire.

"You should go when she isn't expecting you," Dr. Weisman said. "That's the only way you'll know how she actually is."

I nodded, distracted. "Yeah, I'll do that."

My new 'I' was a fragile encroachment, born from the fragments of my disparate homunculi. I could not prove this, I could not be certain, but of this, I formed an important proposition.

III

I stayed up late writing that night. I stayed up late writing after that almost every night. Before, I hadn't really been sleeping but now it became slightly less than superfluous. I tired, but not by much; my thoughts accelerated as long as I whipped them. Epiphanies do not often arrive upon earth, amidst the shadows of replicated faux movements, at least not true epiphanies, very often. I always ridiculed the notion of the spiritual awakening; what I experienced was a phenomenological awakening. It was not just my cognition that had been altered, it was my being there, it was both my 'my' and my 'there.'

Cognition is freedom; cognition is alienation; cognition is necessity.

The following essay I wrote in order to give form to the phenomenology that tortured me. In this way, I could form the first principle of all my work thereafter. Indubitably I understood that, in these propositions, I created no novel insights. To do so, I would have to be God. Per contra, although I could not give birth to any new primary color, what I could do was mediate what already existed under divine constitution for the manifestation of something inspiring. I could not make red. But I'd still befoul it or something of it in my likeness.

The irony of my endeavors also did not escape me. Birth pangs are always cruel, wrought with crying and grinding as a prolegomena to the blooded tears of love at Beauty's feet.

I

For years, now, I have been possessed by an affliction; this possession manifests to me in a particular quality; it is a ubiquitous dread, like an invisible color of gray, and it hurts as if my spirit has consumed smoldering shards of glass. My vision is blurry; no longer can I remember the sensation of silence. Forgive my predilection, but it is my 'first principle.' *Il dolor* is both a chain and a motivation to calculate the potential location of a reverie.

A testimony such as this might be perceived as unbecoming, especially as an introduction; it could be interpreted as the irrational basis for my reflections undercutting any relevance for the 'science' of the radical human project. For this reader, cognition is a meal best served in segregation. To embody it, to present its contents draped in boiled skin, is to force the consumption of something particularly fatty and nauseating. And for those with refined tastes, this is quite detestable; it is the ungodly consummation of dirt.

Mi dispiace. My goal is not to revel in alienation; it is not to fetishize misery; it is to overcome it. To do this, however, I must be honest and present my embodied experience. It is what offers the dimly colored aura to the idea that I am about to present: the hypothesis that radical praxis, rather than surmounting alienation, suffers from a paradox concerning the phenomenon. This notion has bothered me for some time. I present it so that someone else might dethrone it from my consciousness and relieve me from the persecution of a daemon.

II

What is alienation?

For the purposes of exorcism, this question will be answered from the vantage point of the Marxian universe. Alienation, as a phenomenon, cannot be enclosed in this articulation. However, it is this particular perspective that has captured my imagination and warrants these reflections. DaVinci, here, could commiserate with old Father Marx; like the Mona Lisa, the works of the latter have suffered from a great irony of estrangement, having been imitated, interpreted, and transformed by acrimonious equivocation. Certainly, this sin will bear witness, again. Especially since I am forced to be schematic. This phenomenon, in itself, in semblance inescapable, is in a way a damning epistemological proof at first face. This apology, although relevant, is, however, a digression at this point; let us doggy paddle before we engage in glorious and sweeping breaststrokes.

In the *Economic and Philosophic Manuscripts of 1844,* Marx recognized four categories of experience that defined the phenomenon of alienation. He started from the premise of "actual economic fact," from the context of a capitalist political economy. From this premise, Marx posited his first category of alienation as intrinsic to the sensuous process of creation itself in a capitalist economy. Human creation is a process that objectifies human intentions in the external world; however, it is transformed into a process that results in an object foreign, more worthy, and sovereign over the relationally destitute producer under the auspices of capitalist relations. And moreover, Marx posited, this process, by inverting the dynamics of labor, results in the loss of 'realization,' of true 'objectification,' thereby reducing the nature of labor into the production of commodities, which additionally transforms labor into a commodity.

"The worker becomes all the poorer, the more wealth he produces, the more his production increases in power and size. The worker becomes an ever cheaper commodity the more commodities he creates. The *devaluation* of the world of men is in direct proportion to the *increasing value* of the world of things. Labor produces not only commodities; it produces itself and the worker as a *commodity*..."

"This fact expresses merely that the object which labor produces - labor's product - confronts it as *something alien,* as a *power independent* of the producer. The product of labor is labor, which has been embodied in an object, which has become material: it is the *objectification* of labor. Labor's realization is its objectification. Under these economic conditions, this realization of labor appears as *loss of realization* for the workers; objectification as *loss of the object and bondage to it;* appropriation as *estrangement,* as *alienation.*"

We'll illustrate this with our character, Ineffabilis. He is a dour, monstrous sort; despair, frustration, and bondage have given a divine touch to latent dwellings of anger and aggression in his marrow. Nevertheless, he'll serve just fine for our performance.

Ineffabilis exists through a modality of *activity;* his existence is defined by his process of creation, by his process of working on the various materials available to him in order to create something from the visage he possesses in imagination. More specifically, in our moment, Ineffabilis works to make aerospace connectors utilizing a lathe. Ah! How he loves this. The changes he enacts to the form of the aluminum with every meticulous application of the lathe's tools, a nuanced process where every angle, every dimension to the hundredth of an inch makes all the difference to the product's virtue, manifests within the world the *telos* of his spirit. Ineffabilis experiences a validation of his existence, a subtle joy of accomplishment, and encouragement through the voiceless whisper of his labor's end that confirms for him the power of his will.

Now, again, in tension with this primordial phenomenon is its actualization within the uncontrollable system of globalized capital. The connector Ineffabilis made has value; it can be bought and sold in a profit-driven market. Instead of visiting Marx's *Capital,* we'll assume his argued dynamics, where the worth of Ineffabilis' labor power becomes reduced in value amidst a network of other workers and connectors produced *en masse* for profit. The connectors, in this context, possess a value separate from Ineffabilis. Those who buy them and sell them care more about the value of the product than the spirit and worth of the laborer. And not only this but, in their need of controlling for quality for sale, they over-determine the design, the vision, the *telos* of the connector therefore also robbing our dear Ineffabilis of the utility of his imagination.

In this reversal, Ineffabilis *might* grumble in cold irony. The *telos* of his activity has been removed from his control. And the more his creations are valued by others, the more they care for *those* and perceive and treat our dear Ineffabilis as a purchasable means to their ends. No longer is Ineffabilis the master of his object, the connector. It has become a force in its own right, and such a worth has given the little banal, yet intricate inanimate object the semblance of power over *him*. Their 'salability' has been universalized; it has encroached upon his spirit. This facet of alienation communicates a phenomenon of reversal where the process of human labor works towards a self-destructive end. Imagine our Ineffabilis building the very prison in which he is forced to reside.

In this scheme, there is also a subtle, pervasive element. As Marx noted, to realize his life activity, which includes the production of things, Ineffabilis requires the materials of nature; however, these, too, insofar as Ineffabilis produces through the capitalist labor process, have become foreign, owned by the *other* and incorporated into a world-ravenous economic machine. Nature, the 'inorganic body' of Ineffabilis, in all its expansiveness, too becomes a socially separate and antithetical force. And this idea is in relation to the next facet of Marx's exposition.

Proximo, we will discuss Marx's second and third theses—the propositions that human beings suffer not only from estrangement from the things they produce, but that they also suffer from alienation from their life activity in itself, from self-estrangement, and thereby from an estrangement from their 'genetic essence' as well.

The logic is as follows. Human beings, in likeness to other animals, are slaves to their 'inorganic bodies.' To survive, to maintain sustenance, basic requisites must be met: eating, drinking, and sleeping, etc. To continue living, there is no way around this. However, what distinguishes humans (although not *perfectly*) is the capacity for *telos,* for rational agency, and outside of the bounds of pure necessity. For example, a human can utilize and hone his or her life activity towards aesthetic ends without any purpose of sustenance. And here, within this capability, this power, is the (questionable) embryo of freedom; this, for our purposes, is the qualia that isolate humanness. Outside of a few anomalies, no animals possess this quality in their being. This teleological activity, guided by reason, relatively unfettered by banal material laws, is what is posited to be the eminent force in human ontology.

Such beauty, however, becomes a harrowing seducer when raised in the house of a profiteering overlord. Prostitution colors pulchritude in strokes of shade, just the same as sex, with all the potential for spiritual endowments, can leave an oppressive vapidity when experienced in the context of coercion, whether it be of social or corporeal form. The dispossession of the means of production from the broad masses, as eluded to previously, transforms the gift of humanity into something severed, something separate and alien, and owned by other forces. The appropriation of nature and the entire plethora of machinery, making them unavailable except through the coercion of wage-labor that starvation and insecurity inevitably corroborate, is what turns 'human productive activity' into *labor,* into *work.* This materialized *reduction* (abstraction) of productive human activity and its appropriation by another is the essence self-estrangement.

Another pertinent facet concerns another form of reversal; in this context, one "lives to work," his or her life activity becomes defined (reductively and abstractly) by their alienated labor. The most pernicious aspect of this reversal is the mutation of what constitutes the 'essence' of humanity, the capability, the power and will towards freedom, the qualia of rational-creative *telos,* into a process experienced as base animal slavery; and just conversely, this social relation defines what more truly is animal, the fulfillment of basic needs of sustenance, as *human freedom.* A laborer's 'free' time is occupied by eating, drinking, and sleeping—and these acts become preeminent sources of jubilance! Certainly, this schemata isn't naively representational—human beings socialize, have sex, and so forth; however, these activities become *marginal* in a sphere where humanity's cardinal attribute dominates in a type of banally suppressive *camera obscura.*

"The relation of labor to the *act of production* within the *labor* process. This relation is the relation of the worker to his own activity as an alien activity not belonging to him; it is activity as suffering, strength as weakness, begetting as emasculating, the worker's *own* physical and mental energy, his personal life - for what is life but activity? - as an activity which is turned against him, independent of him and not belonging to him. Here we have *self-estrangement,* as previously we had the estrangement of the *thing.*"

I do not believe we require Ineffabilis to dance for us, here. But he wishes too. He would like us to see how he suffers. Old unspeakable arises before dawn to sit in traffic, dredge through the production of connectors following an authoritatively pre-ordained blueprint, down to the detail, day by day, only to sit through more traffic. What he creates through his work is genial; unfortunately, it just isn't *his* genius. He does not share in the ownership of his activity just as he does not share in the ownership of his product. Moreover, Ineffabilis socializes at work, but only minimally and rather constrainedly; here, all laughs are like bubbles arising from those who drown. He crosses the threshold of his door by early evening.

This is where his freedom begins. There are only a few hours left in his day to maintain his sanity and health. A huff of gruff inaudible mumbles, he sits for dinner in stony quiet. With a deep exhale, he eats his meal: an anti-depressant as entrée, a bowl of spaghetti as a side. Emaciated, Ineffabilis is forced to feign his real love for his faux bastard children. He brushes his teeth before fornicating with his partner for approximately five minutes. His motions, if they could be categorized as such, liken more to the mechanical sequence of his lathe in predictably rigid retractions and pumps. Lubricant is required. Noises—they are made. Machinery; it ceases. Eventually, there is sleep, but such an experience squirms beneath the shadow of a mal-anticipated morning.

Furthermore, as per Marx, within the confines of modern social relations, human beings are also alienated from their 'species-being,' their *multifaceted possibility,* their *irreducible quality of incalculable potential to become, to be*—and this is the third aspect of alienation common to experience, which follows as a consequence of these relations.

"It is just in his work upon the objective world. Therefore, that man really proves himself to be a *species-being.* This production is his active species-life. Through this production, nature appears as *his* work and his reality. The object of labor is, therefore, the *objectification of man's species-life*: for he duplicates himself not only, as in consciousness, intellectually, but also actively, in reality, and therefore he sees himself in a world that he has created. In tearing away from man the object of his production, therefore, estranged labor tears from him his *species-life,* his real objectivity as a member of the species and transforms his advantage over animals into the disadvantage that his inorganic body, nature, is taken from him…Similarly, in degrading spontaneous, free activity to a means, estranged labor makes man's species-life a means to his physical exist-ence…The consciousness which man has of his species is thus transformed by estrangement in such a way that species[-life] becomes for him a means."

Understanding this aspect of Herr Marx's conception requires a foray into dialectic; in so doing this, the previous points may also be further (artificially) illuminated, especially the phenomenon of abstraction/reduction eminent in the second facet of estrangement. Marx, here, is re-stating the second facet of estrangement under the auspices of another vector. The *abstraction,* the *reduction* of human productive activity into labor (wage-labor, coerced production, where the process is predicated upon the context where nature, the constructed means of production, and the product of rational creativity are owned by an alien force and/or possess value and power above and over dear Ineffabilis), transforms the factor that singularizes humanity into a means for crude individual reproduction. In other words, what Herr Marx takes to be the *universal essence* of human existence, rational telos, is reversed and subjugated and delimited into a medium for the material existence of the slave. Thus, in addition to representing self-estrangement, this very same phenomenon also signifies the individual's estrangement from his or her 'genetic' essence. Human activity, 'spontaneous, free activity,' a phenomenon embryonically polygon, and one that escapes taxonomy loses its dimensions to the schemata of the blueprint and the mill. Ineffabilis has already demonstrated these dynamics, as per the tragic reversal. To add to his performance, however, let us reemphasize that Ineffabilis is an aerospace worker—and more precisely, a lathe operator. This identity, predicated on contemporary social relations, *defines* the majority of his life, in an ontic and symbolic sense. His family and friends certainly arrive shortly after in time and space, the ensemble of their relations constrained very similarly by the extrapolations of the shop. *Contra* the fantasies of Ineffabilis, however, his predispositions, his skills, the more profound visages of his imagination—they are all truly ineffable; for the cold requisites of modern *labor* have long stamped out their fledgling flames. Perhaps embers remain, but one cannot discern the realm of architectural possibility from squandered and spoiled supplies. Here, the state of freedom is sundered and in a manner more pernicious than the apparent level of generality concerning the worker's chain to his or her owner; while the two levels exist in mediation, the more insidious level of sundering finds its locality in the *spirit*. A bond to another can be broken; however, it remains to be seen how justice can be restored to the soul.

Lastly, Marx posited a final dimension of estrangement—the estrangement of human beings from one another. And again, this facet of estrangement is determined by the logic of previous propositions. We have seen how human beings are alienated from the products of their labor, becoming devalued in inversed correlation, how this process and its basis, therefore, relates to the estrangement of productive activity itself, and consequently, how this phenomenon signifies a loss, a reversal of human powers, where individuals, as part of the species, become realizations of emaciating *abstractions*. What results from this is that human beings would likewise be estranged from one another— that they would experience the other, and reflectively, the self, as reductions, as abstractions, as devalued automatons.

"...An immediate consequence of the fact that man is estranged from the product of his labor, from his life activity, from his species-being, is the *estrangement of man from man*. When man confronts himself, he confronts the *other* man. What applies to a man's relation to his work, to the product of his labor and to himself, also holds of a man's relation to the other man, and to the other man's labor and object of labor..."

"...In fact, the proposition that man's species-nature is estranged from him means that one man is estranged from the other, as each of them is from man's essential nature...The estrangement of man, and in fact every relationship in which man [stands] to himself, is realized and expressed only in the relationship in which a man stands to other men...Hence within the relationship of estranged labor each man views the other in accordance with the standard and the relationship in which he finds himself as a worker."

Ineffabilis will save his dances for another act. What is clear here is that our dear gentleman creature, in confronting other human beings, does not experience them as such; instead, he perceives the semblances of dimensionalities made preeminent by the social relations of capital. He perceives *abstract beings*. And his interactions with them, which reflect and reproduce his own existence, are mediated by a simplex. Polygons become square; concrete possibilities, those innumerable expectant mothers, experience death before the hour of labor. What is born is still; it is not human, it is something humoresque, lacking in the requisite worth of what is good, agreeable, and closer to harmonious.

III

How does the radical lock arms with this phenomenon?

The war on estrangement seems to have different fields, which can be conceptualized variably depending on the required emphases. Exploiting and laboring classes within the context of the world imperialist system polarize the primary field for this schema. Since alienation, in this *espiritus,* is predicated upon these relations, the first-order objective is the abolition of this system. The secondary field seems to be defined by radical forces (be they working class and/or cadre) and mezzo ones (relatively localized elites, owners, and institutions that mediate this plane with the primary one) in polarization. Next, the tertiary field of polarization seems to be organizational—the field where distinct and separate radical organizations contend for the loyalty of constituents in order to construct a political movement with enough accrued force to shift relations in the first and second fields. The fourth field of warfare is the intra-organizational plane, where cadre and/or members of different radical blocs within it act in contention with other related and/or allied forces to determine the ontology and vector of the whole so that this total organism may aptly determine the movement in congruence with its visage. Fifth in order is the field that is defined by the relation between the organization, its representatives, and the individual member—in this plane, the avatars of the organization exert power over the singular in order to determine his or her spirit so that the total organism might achieve greater Arête. And finally, the sixth field of battle is intra-individual, where heteronomous beings strive towards the dialectical negation of the self in order to manifest the radical *espiritus* in persona with or without the determinations of other human forces.

This matrix is incomplete, yet nevertheless suitable for the moment. These fields, which are vast in potential and complimented by undisclosed dimensions, are inner-determining mediations that form a concatenation of events, a reflexive and dynamic open system.

We will focus on the last field—the sixth field—that serves to theorize the process whereby a human being engages in activities that purport to approach the surmounting of estrangement as a phenomenon, and more singularly and immediately, his or her own disposition and experience. Ineffabilis will serve us once again.

Ineffabilis, our lathe operator, has already demonstrated his estrangement. He is exploited at work. He labors for approximately seven to eight hours a day, at least, making aerospace connectors that are pre-determined in design. These connectors, the results of his labor, appreciate in value; their sale consequences in the reproduction, the invigoration, of his economic penance. What makes our dear Ineffabilis a human, his capacities for rationally directed imagination for the sake of creation, have been transfixed into a base utility. He is poor and his fantasies, his dreams, they are destitute. And more, the reverberations of such enthrallment pejoratively delimit his relations with his family, his friends, with others in general.

What could make him free has instead been turned into a medium for slavery; conversely, the events and activities that link him to creatures have become the markers of his freedom.

In essence, Ineffabilis, at this point, is a heteronomous being; his ontology is an ensemble and social, determined by the hegemony, ideologies, and habits of contemporary social relations. When he sees an entity at work, he perceives a *co-worker,* keeps him or her at a distance, is careful what he does and says, a partial relation based upon a competitive factory system of production within the global economy. When he experiences his partner, who is female, he experiences a *wife,* and possesses particular, albeit modern expectations concerning her behavior—and this category of perception, according to our radical corpus, is predicated upon a culture of sexism arisen from class distinctions and commandeered by contemporary relations. He witnesses a human entity of a particular phenotype, and this occurrence is modulated through the prism of difference, of race, due to his habituation within a certain temporal-spatial dimension following the birth of racism in the colonial United States. His co-worker gets fired for ruining too many connectors, but Ineffabilis cowers out of concern for his job, security, and family. An innocent man gets executed because of his skin color; Ineffabilis hides in front of his monitor, in quiet and tired indignation.

No matter what the event, in fact, Ineffabilis generally realizes that a certain cognition, emotion, or behavior manifests within his being, and quite automatically. But if it is automatic, is it he? If it is not him, who is it, or from what force does it originate? Automation is alien, at least when unrefined by the psyche, when lacking in conscious self-determination. Thus, Ineffabilis is a heteronomous being—a persona determined by *other* forces, which are predicates of capitalism. Ineffabilis is a thrall. This insight plagues him; he potently desires agency. It is this affective cognition that motivates our dear gentleman monster to engage in the fight for a more authentic and just existence.

Newly incorporated into a socialist organization, Ineffabilis begins to appropriate his freedom by consciously employing his human faculties. He attends meetings to participate in discourses on alternative comprehensions of nature and social relations. He reads texts that expose him to meanings, which are new *to him,* that empower him to reflect not only upon them, but also upon his own history and disposition. His phenomenology shifts. Now, he perceives his automatic phenomena as determinations of an oppressive regime and system. Thus commences the process towards 'self-mastery,' towards the 'construction of agency,' towards the abolition (albeit imperfect and incomplete without movement in additional fields) of his enthralled elements. Integrally, thus begins the re-habituation of Ineffabilis through his participation in a behavior and politics of radical alterity, predicated upon the radical *espiritus.* His ultimate goal is to help produce, through his transformational activism, a revolutionary movement to destroy the objective foundation of human estrangement. However, to enable movements in the fields necessary to achieve this negation, Ineffabilis holds in intention another notion— namely, that he must become, in spirit, congruent with the visage, with the specter of the revolution that motivates him in haunt.

Deo et regi fidelis, Ineffabilis does a dish. Let us attempt to sketch the experience of this phenomenon, regardless of its brutishness, beginning at the line of demarcation that marks his penurious freedom. In order to achieve this sketch, it seems like I must contrast Ineffabilis *nuovo* with his bedeviled antecedent.

Ineffabilis the First, the Monstrous, arrives home from work with a particular complex of sentiments. He is fatigued from standing, lifting, and straining for eight hours or more; he is frustrated from tedium; his fantasies, be they sexual and/or egoistic conflict with the cruel facts of the matter; the last thing he wishes to do is think, affect, converse, nurture—these desires and capacities dwell, but they are circumvented by a nature seemly harrowed. A pure witticism, he crosses his chest as he crosses *his* threshold. To the spritely and spirited cry of children, he winces. Once again, spaghetti cools upon a table besieged by cantankerous hobgoblins and their aging mistress Wiccan. She smiles at him shortly. It feels like a condemnation. He is late, the kitchen is dirty, the *wife* is slovenly with bags and wrinkles (she raises children for a living, other than her own, no doubt). It is *his* turn to do a dish.

Our esteemed Unspeakable refuses, of course, and acidic spits soon resume their dissolution of their sacrosanct vows. At any rate, let us isolate some of these cognitions, emotions, and behaviors before moving forward, since, so often times, the qualia of our person is defined through them.

Ineffabilis is fatigued, in disposition—depressed—however, perhaps not clinically. This chronic physiological-psychological status delineates the range of his emotions. When home from work, he often times feels like he is incapable of a smile and his tiredness renders his affect vulnerable to agitation. The irritation of his wife and/or children easily paints his face, although the brightness of their smiles finds such terrain slippery. When the pressure of fulfilling some additional labor about the house locates his person, in his state, he experiences the following thoughts: that he is *not* working further and that his *wife* is not doing her job. A history of conflict over this sequence of phenomena also adds an electrifying anxiety to his being; to his tiredness, it adds a draining vibration, to his thoughts, it adds an uncanny speed, disorganization, and edge, and to his feelings, it does the same, further enabling his dour aura. Certain behaviors result—our Unspeakable sparks and/or participates in a fight with his partner.

Thus, we have a limited reflexive structure: tiredness, rooted in laborious expense, gives rise to an aggravated categorical phenomenology, an anxious despair; this conjoins with a conceptual framework where a female partner is interpreted as wife, with subsequent domestic duties; the unfulfilled domestic task exacerbates his discomfort and results in a critical projection onto her being; an argument arises, mediated by a long string of similar events; in this conflict, Ineffabilis' negativity becomes extrapolated, and, as per the radical *espiritus,* this phenomenon reifies the etiological social relations by burying them beneath the rubble of superficial domestic squabbles, which are not wholly superficial.

In short, Ineffabilis, estranged from his species-being, becomes estranged from his partner, his wife, an event determined by a system of gender roles and his projected emotional abuse, and the semblance that materializes from this sequence makes invisible the pernicious 'hand of the market.'

Enter the redeterminations of the radical *espiritus,* which exist in cognitive and behavioral form. Now, we can try to understand the new Ineffabilis. First and foremost, through a process of education (reading, study groups, innumerable discussions with others) he has learned that human estrangement, as understood, is inexorably linked with oppressive gender relations, with the marginalization of women through categorical domestic labor and roles. Moreover, he has learned that often times, the chauvinism and immaturity of men contributes to this facet of alienation, visibly and invisibly, consciously and unconsciously; and even more, that this alienation of women, of the other, results in his very own oppression, exploitation, and ultimately, his very own disempowerment, etc. The category of *wife,* with its traditional archeology of categories and notions, enables him to empower the system, 'in the last analysis.'

So, yes—Ineffabilis does a dish, and this is the resulting behavioral revolution, although this 'step' need not precede the other. In order to struggle with his internalized sexism, with the culture of thoughts and behaviors that he fulfilled without conscious choice, and in order to better realize himself as a more holistic and revolutionary human being, Ineffabilis, although tired, also tends more to the children when he gets home. He forces smiles, becomes more tender at least outwardly. No longer does he expect sex. Anxious despair he replaces with vibrant hope and a satisfaction that comes with lesser degrees of cognitive dissonance; in place of *wife* he rewrites *comrade;* instead of a schema of abstention, contention, and strife in terms of domestic divisions of labor, Ineffabilis fights for the deconstruction of such divisions of labor for the purposes of making ontic the dissolution of gender.

Of course, this cognitive-behavioral revolution is not limited to the home. At work, Ineffabilis also utilizes his education in the catechisms of the radical spirit to transform his being and world. Whilst before, he saw work as no place for intimate connections, he now engages himself more, socially, under the auspices of a different motif. The goal of recruitment and social transformation of others in *telos,* he purposefully establishes relationships with coworkers. When a racist or sexist joke is made, he doesn't laugh— and this, although minuscule, is a quark of revolutionary action. When the boss walks by, he scowls and endears a rude witticism with intentional content as well in this new light. No longer does he compete to produce out of fear or pride.

Due to a 'law of uneven development,' or some such, our esteemed Unspeakable also learns to filter out co-workers and friends who might have less potential or are outwardly corrupted by capitalism. Finite in his capacity and time, he focuses on those individuals who present to him with more congruence or potential congruence with the radical spirit. Upon them, he labors. Our Ineffabilis recruits. This emboldens him. Praxis—the unity of theory and practice—ever infinite in process, nevertheless progresses; the more he labors upon himself, the more he works upon others; the more he works upon others, the more he also works upon himself. A thousand years of civil war, Marx said.

Quite truly, this process is nothing other than the process of self-negation, in its dialectical sense. With the visage of a radical *telos* in mind, Ineffabilis works to destroy his aged and automatic self in order to more effectively and authentically transform others. Simultaneously, he seeks to construct his new identity alongside his universe— Ineffabilis the Thrall seeks to reflexively produce Ineffabilis the Rebel—and this identity is a progeny of an ideal, born of its specter, just the same as the biblical man was manifested in the shade of God.

IV

This process is teleological, although not *necessarily* in the messianic and eschatological sense. Put plainly, the radical answer to human estrangement is defined by its essence as rational, goal-directed behavior. Just as the revolutionary seeks the abolition of modern social relations for the sake of developing a more egalitarian order, the revolutionary agent, in the most elementary field of struggle, seeks the abolition of the modern preordained self for the ends of achieving a more holistic and just individual essence.

Where does the visage of this essence, this desired *ends*, originate? Our Ineffabilis internalized it through education. He absorbed *ideas* through discourses, through readings, through writing and the phenomena of conversation. For the staunch materialist, the point here is not an idealist one, it is one that emphasizes that our Ineffabilis' phenomenological transformation possessed roots in his ideological-behavioral reconstruction, which, ultimately, has its own roots in radical dogmas and their exegeses. And these dogmas, though bearing the appearances of gods, suffer from the basic and irrefutable fact that they were born from the flesh of women and men.

In other words, these ideas are formed from systems of *categories*. Here a caveat requires attention even if it has become annoyingly commonplace. When we name something, it establishes a meaning. Categorical construction is the building of a house. Before the house was there, there was only nature in its infinite colors—the sky, the clouds, the grasses, the flowers, the rocks, rabbits, the snakes, the poly-symphony. With the construction of the house, however, there are consequences. Not only are certain facets of the scene literally covered and obscured, but also our focus becomes enchanted by the architecture of the house. Certainly, this scene need not be lesser in beauty; and more, many may project hearth, security, control into this humanization of nature. Such a construction could also result in a novel and fecund reading of other natural phenomena. Nevertheless, with this house, there are also losses. From our determinations, from our mediated vantage point, we become blind to what the house conceals. This is a conundrum of epistemology, for which the dialectic is utilized for a delusion of amelioration. By naming, we construct; by naming, we negate. *Nihil est simul et inventum et perfectum.*

What happens, then, when we apply the art of naming, of categorical construction and application, to our dear mascot-monster, Sir Ineffabilis?

Let us take an adventure into the psychotherapeutic dungeon to elucidate this point. The clinical process is predicated on an integral motif of the Enlightenment: control. For mental health, as per radicalism, the important subset of this theme is self-determination. In place of a rigorous exploration, let us suggest an aphorism—the modern act (and even the 'postmodern' one) is a strike against natural, e.g. 'unconscious,' process. For the radical, an individual is a naturally occurring heteronomous composite of incommensurable qualities. A person is born and raised in a family, community, and society; 'pre-existing' relations inseminate this individual with cognitions, values, and practices that eventually blossom into a troublesome cacophony. The act of rebellion, of self-determination, is posited to be the process where this individual decides to reformulate his or her being in not only a manner that is *chosen* but in a manner that is empowering.

Clinical therapy shares this quality in spirit. The person entering a session arrives as a predetermined, relatively unreflective being in strife. When he or she finishes with the clinician, the goal is that he or she better understands their posited essence in addition to achieving a higher degree of agency. This new disposition is hoped to further enable cognitive, affective, and practical/behavioral self-transformation for whatever ends.

The first act of developing this particular phenomenon of control is the production of a clinical assessment through the labor of a therapeutic alliance. Importantly, the creation of such a clinical product is a dynamic illocutionary-perlocutionary process. The clinician, in partnership with the client, performs the role of extrinsic consciousness. This partnership and role are, of course, inescapably complicated by the reactivity of orientations, but this is, for now, irrelevant. In this process, the clinician interacts with the client holistically; he or she asks an array of questions to assemble information while promoting reflection. Although a gross simplification, when this process nears completion, the clinician will present a nascent, conceptualized totality of the client's 'biopsychosocial' disposition and history for corroboration and/or alteration.

In this phenomenon between two human beings, the process is arguably equal if not greater to the ends, the completed assessment, because it is in this process that the client, the embodied consciousness seeking understanding and empowerment, creates *statements, propositions,* that, firstly, *describe* the self, thereby intentionally manifesting an incipient picture/comprehension of the self that is both affirmative and critical, and that secondly, *declare the need for negation and/or amelioration,* an act of intended force, which is the basis for the development of perlocutionary acts. These two categories of speech acts inherent in this process cannot be so formally abstracted, however; variably, in this process, an illocutionary act *is* a perlocutionary act, for the construction of an ideation, and even one without articulated intention of force, can in and of itself become reflexively causal and therefore actualized.

For the sake of brevity, a detailed journey into Ineffabilis' assessment must be limited to a few basic points. When I first met the creature, he didn't completely recognize himself in the mirror; and furthermore, he represented a complete mystery to his onlooker, this esteemed clinical psychotherapist—at this point, there were no words for him, no knowledge to symbolize his ontology.

A few initial notations of some signs brought an initial discourse to life. He was scruffy, had purple bags under his eyes; he walked slowly and rigidly in a manner that paralleled the flat expression on his face. When he said, "I'm Ineffabilis," his words carried a forced and dour energy. An acknowledgment of these things, which appeared normal to him since he lived with himself every day, manifested a brief expression of shock and perplexity, which of course preceded an uncomfortably humorous admission that he was sleepless, frustrated, and unhappy.

From here, Ineffabilis talked. Stimulated by my questions and cues, Ineffabilis posited that he was "emotionally abusive and oppressive" to his family because he was a miserable soul. "Work is killing me. I want to spend time with my family, but there is something wrong with me. I'm always irritable, and I hate it." He also disclosed, after being asked about his earlier life, which included family life, that his father often screamed at him and assaulted him—and importantly, that this caused him to live in a consistent hyper vigilant state since he always had to be aware of his father's location for reasons of preparation, preemption, and child-like safety. Before this therapist could make *any* notation, he added, "I was raised in a very traditional household. I guess I've learned that a man should behave a certain way."

The conversation continued. Before long, Ineffabilis, in response to questions pertaining to his general health, disclosed that he suffered from chronic pain in his lower back, that he was hypertensive, and that he felt like he experienced heart palpitations. From here, perhaps because he associated all psychological symptoms with physiological ones, he similarly stated that he often felt restless, generally uncomfortable—that this sabotaged his ability to relax and sleep. When it got really bad, he would sweat and cringe as if he was experiencing a heart attack. Here, Ineffabilis trembled as he spoke, communicating with a punctuation of intensity that appeared to bury tears: he experienced paroxysms of extraneous terror regularly throughout the week, sometimes before work, sometimes during and/or after dinner. "I finally saw a doctor, but he said it wasn't a heart attack. I don't know what's going on, but I feel like I'm falling apart. Why am I like this?"

Though crude, we have now developed an incipient ideology concerning our dear Mr. Unspeakable. Per his reflected psychosocial history, we can justify the utilization of *abused* and *fearful/anxious* as descriptors that color the trajectory of his development. Similarly, we can also hypothesize a 'traditional' cultural factor that seemed to delineate his comprehension of social relations. These variables, in relation to his current modality of life, which is largely defined by a work environment that he presented first as an external destructive force, the problematic of his relations with family and the contradiction between his desires and his practices herein, his medical problems, which could be pertinent determined, causal and/or exacerbating factors, and his current experience of self-loathing, generally, already give us a fecund complex. Ineffabilis, formerly a mystery, has become somewhat explicable.

Now, Ineffabilis has a name—he is Effable. And from this foundation, the therapeutic alliance can employ reason to infer a suitable *telos* for the alleged process of metamorphosis. Controversies of psychotropic medication aside, Mr. Effable decides with the aid of his extrinsic consciousness that he wishes to redefine the architecture of his cognition and related forces. No longer does he wish to perceive his partner through a traditional prism. He will work towards experiencing her differently through a series of cognitive exercises as he forces himself to participate in daily household tasks. Moreover, the new Effable man also desires to master his automatic physiological responses through the utilization of biofeedback and various relaxation techniques. As per his work, Mr. Effable envisions himself as more upright, with a spine. The dictates of his work environment, he swears, will someday fall upon him with no more weight than necessary; to do this, he'll contract with himself to rely more and more upon his comrades at work for support, which will be operationalized by the countable occurrences per week that he positively interacts with them, for certainly, they can empathize with his experience. This union, it is hypothesized, will render the workplace more hospitable and *less* destructive. Though far from revolutionary, this change could represent a shift in the 'war of position' to enable more movement.

Put succinctly, Ineffabilis has become Effable insofar as he has been defined through an intricate baseline history as *patriarchal,* as *anxious,* and as *estranged.* From this, the visage of a new human being in the future is construed. This Effable man *to be* is defined to be more *egalitarian, tranquil,* and *whole/empowered.* The goal of manifesting this disposition is what delineates the process of transformation. All activity, all the events that become steps and/or stages in the process of cognitive, affective, and behavioral reconstruction, must be congruent and harmonious with this end. In this, they are, in form and essence, defined by what has yet to exist. The flesh, again, must yield to the contours of the ethereal born from its imagination.

V

Regression to our earlier caveat now presents us with a new vantage point for exploration. Ineffabilis, at least in relative essence and identity, was, before the therapeutic process of assessment, autological in an *ontic* sense, although not in a semantic or cultural one. *Per contra,* after the process, after the creation of the assessment as product, Ineffabilis became Effable—and 'Effable' likens to our caveat of the house. Certain categories were constructed in order to communicate our dear monster's posited essence; and from these categories, what *needs to be,* a future ontology, was inferred—and summarily, to these projections, the ontic must change.

From these categories, we 'learned' things about our favorite dancing man-beast, certain phenomena became comprehensible and fecund; however, what has been concealed and/or fallen into invisibility outside the horizon of our intentionality? This question possesses no simple answer.

Clinicians posit the following two propositions. One fundamental axiom is that the clinician, as the extrinsic consciousness, must remain where the client is experientially; consequently, the clinician knows no more and can work with no more or less than what the unspeakable before them presents for labor. The second axiom is that the creature, as per his or her autological and ontic nature, per his or her origin, *truly is ineffable.* No entity, besides those deemed divine, possesses flawless self-knowledge. All mortal entities are therefore made mysterious in *ontic* quality. In the ontic realm, *we are all Ineffabilis.*

Recall the proposition that modern estrangement results from the abstract reduction of human essence. Any human being is intrinsically polygon in being/becoming. From any relative moment of maturity, based on the material presented, past potential for development or the lack thereof can be induced, although, of course, without certainty. Beings arrive at a contemporary disposition through the 'dialectical' negation of such embryonic qualia.

The life world enacts contradictory forces upon all beings; in a moment, a being is *developed,* or rather, an event transpires that enhances one qualia and/or diminishes another, giving rise to more potential development. However, in this same moment, a being seems *abstracted* in that this event delimits further development in a manner adverse to the ineffable polygon. Or, rather, at one theoretical point, an individual entity possessed *innumerable possibilities with parallel trajectories, ad infinitum.* The further this being travels through time-space, the *less diffuse these trajectories become.* They become relatively abstract beings as they become more 'concrete' when considered beside their genetic structure.

If these propositions are accepted, and all beings are ineffable in the ontic realm, and this is their 'naïve/savage essence,' then the Effable, the *ontological product* of labor upon the self, especially when considered in tandem with the ideological materials inexorably born and owned by individual and/or collective others, becomes something relatively *separate, alien,* and *destructive* upon every Ineffabilis. For the first product, the assessed self, is predicated upon a comprehension refracted from an extrinsic consciousness, and the second, ethereal projection from this first proof, to which the ontic Ineffabilis requires further molding, is the creative/destructive actualization of this ultimately foreign ideal. Ineffabilis weakens, becomes only further hidden and/or destroyed as the product, the Effable, grows stronger.

Secondly, by our same original comprehension of estrangement, the *activity* by which Ineffabilis recreates himself into the Effable is one similarly contaminated, one similarly alien. Put succinctly and plainly, his activities, which include all the acts and events of discourse (reading, talking, writing) and all the shifts in behavior, instead of being determined by him, are instead mediated by hegemonic dogmas, regardless of partisanship. For the psychotherapeutic alliance, all activities are pre-contained within the controlled boundaries of the clinical institution, and with all its repertoires. Ineffabilis might partake and of his own accord; however, this does not relinquish his estrangement from the means.

The sublation of the third thesis concerning estrangement, that of a being's alienation from their 'species-being,' has already been described in the phenomenon of development/abstraction. All events that enhance, that realize potential, suffer from the paradox that they simultaneously delimit and destroy *alternate potentials in greater number.* As per this logic, *the very utilization of the logos, of reason, and its application to the ontic Ineffabilis, the very 'realization' of a power that isolates/defines humanity, results in only the Effable, in the abstraction, the reduction, of women and men.* And when this reason and the archaeology/architecture of categories it necessarily utilizes are born from the inexorably flawed and embodied minds of women and men, and these categories are employed (because they must be) to manifest the visage of a *telos,* and the ontic Ineffabilis is bound to its basic complex dimensions, and convinced to submit to its delineations, the result is self-negation with all its violence. This labor differs in the sense that it does not reduce a human being's genetic activity to the base utility of survival; however, it most certainly fulfills the shared motif of *delimitation and reversal.*

And lastly, this process, by extension, also results in the projection of abstractions onto other women and men. Ineffabilis, at first, experienced a wife (a reduction of an Ineffabilis); now, he experiences a *partner* (a perhaps more culturally favorable, yet nevertheless a reduction all the same).

VI

Finally, we arrive at the paradox concerning the radical challenge to alienation. Up until this point, we have explored the psychotherapeutic process. True enough, as was previously articulated, the radical challenge cannot be conflated with the latter. They are different phenomena. Unfortunately, though, this is not to the benefit of the radical notion—for the psychotherapeutic method is far superior in sophistication where *they are* similar—and this, also, is what partially makes it different.

Where, in general, the psychotherapeutic profession draws upon large continents of knowledge and experience concerning human existence in its multifarious facets, the radical tradition remains constrained by the basic complexes of 'Marxist' political economy. With all its flaws—and this is true—the clinician considers development in a far more global context; he or she considers any number of biopsychosocial and spiritual variables while constructing their Effable. And yet, the contemporary radical, in loyalty to former exegeses, mostly reduces human behavior to *ideology, economy,* and *politics.* By exposing the paradox of the clinical process, then, I have summarily also hoped to expose any methodological challenge to estrangement that is simpler in its phenomenology. This is mathematics. If a function that is greater in trajectory than another converges to naught, then by necessity, so does the lesser one that rests in its shadow.

At this point, I'll cease to be coy. This is the daemon that I wish to be exorcised—that nagging voice, that deplorable thought, that commonplace naysaying that human alienation, at least in its herein described universe, is the result of nature, and in extension, logos. That the radical project, although hypothesized as a cure, is but a sublation and continuation of the phenomenon, inevitably and indubitably. For the elimination of capitalist social relations would not relieve the haunting of this experience.

Solitudinem fecerunt, pacem appelunt!

IV

The life world, the ontic world, became distant. I navigated it from far away. Eating was a burden, the same as sleep. I didn't care to shave. I continued to shower and take care of myself—my vanity was still of importance, at least to God— but I let my facial hair grow, only cleaning it up every so often as a subtle whisper instructed—not a voice, a disembodied thought. I did not hear voices. I heard thoughts—streams of them, flowing so loudly, serenely, and wearingly. Had I a way to categorize their essence, their origins? I did not, so perhaps they were voices of the dead, or some such. I do not think the wisest and most genial cognitive scientist could prove me wrong—he or she could only try and dissuade me abductively.

I was failing to master myself. I was failing to master my clients—what change had been wrought? Rage and despotism named me.

For this reason, I continued to labor. This was the sublation of my postmodernism, the reclamation of being and thought. Objects, subjects, they were categories of Plato's cave. I could come to accept myself intuitively in a world transcending basic effect and logic. Here was the last step in the dance, where cognition again became freedom, but more so through its necessity, where I enacted therapy reflexively to force my evolution. This is where psychotherapy can attain a position of maneuver and power. Individual thoughts, concatenations of thoughts, of feelings, and behaviors only obtain significance contextually. By bringing to attention these individual phenomena or these strings of phenomena, the clinician, and/or client delineates them meaningfully and alters them at will through the manifestation of metacognition, of 'Dasein.' To think that this is accomplished mechanically, in light of the disjointedness and stupidity of the meta-I, is a proposition made in error. There is a reproduction that is anarchic. These commodities of therapeutic labor, perverted as they may be, enter the ideology/being of the clinician and/or client; they affect akin to free radicals, traveling back to the genetic structure of the web of belief to alter its disposition through a method beyond anything utterable.

First principles arise from intuition. First principles are the foundation of reason. Whether intuition and intentionality can be conflated is not clear, but what is clear is the inefficacy of the 'I,' constituted from the 'they,' and the Promethean and despotic nature of the meta-I. A truer revolution, adhering to a new being, is the negation of the intuitive. In this way, new first principles could arise and from there, the visage of a more authentic 'I,' and one capable of surpassing even its antecedent meta-being, could pass into existence as an autological one.

This being had to affect; it had to be imperial. If this phenomenon is singular, it is psychotic and unrealized. And here apparently Hegel was still my master—and a grand example that I still suffered from alien fantasies. To become indigenous, my new intuition had to engage in murder; it required the submission, the negation of others. And here I was haunted by paradox.

Outside of God, it seemed that the only true being possible was the one whose consciousness had been destroyed.

But was this not Kirilov?

CHAPTER TWELVE

I

Everything is slow. Nothing is worthy of mention.

II

I'm at work. I barely get there. I'm late. My boss looks at me but says nothing. He knows. Everyone knows.

III

I am slumped. I get a call. It's Napoleon's sister. There was a bag of methamphetamine in his room. He's throwing a fit. He's red, she says. I tell her I'm coming later and to stay calm.

IV

I get another call. He's struck their mother. The police are called. They never arrive. She's crying. She wants my help. I tell her to call 911 again. There's silence. I can hear masculine shrieks in the background. She whispers that he has a knife.

V

I speak to Napoleon. He tells me that he is Lord Napoleon the Third, the new lamb and Son of God and Satan and that he has attained close to near perfect clarity and perfection. He is no longer depressed, he says. He speaks fast, too fast for me to understand. He screams at me when I ask him if he's used methamphetamine. He says I will be raped and he knows who I am. He's always known who I am, he says. I am a chameleon, and he will not be controlled. He will finish his great purification. I will suffer.

VI

I update my boss. He looks tired and dried. He doesn't even look like Paul anymore; he dresses differently. He tells me to call the police in his area directly and after confirming that they are responding, to arrive afterwards for my safety. I do so. They ask me what I want. They locate the record of the call. They ask who I am. I tell them. The operator and then a different person tell me that they are responding. They sounded dry, uncaring, even annoyed that I've asked them to do their job.

VII

I feel like I'm fading. The crisis gives me a shot of epinephrine.

VIII

I forgot the sister's name. I think it's Cassandra. She looks beautiful. Her eyes are swollen and itchy from tears. She sees me walking from my car. I cannot help but feel draggy but I walk fast. I see Napoleon in the back of a police car. He's glaring at me with wide eyes in furious awe and zeal. As Cassandra reaches me, I extend my hand and touch hers. I wish I could feel warm, but at least I can look warm. She hugs me. Napoleon watches. I see him wince and grow angrier.

"He'll be alright," I say. "Now, we can do what is best for him. He needs to be conserved."

I said those words without thinking. "Yes," she says, but without knowing what I am saying.

I spend the next twenty-five or so minutes speaking with sheriffs, not police. I guess I did not see a police car. I saw a sheriff car. I confirm his diagnosis for them and request psych hospitalization. I ask them to take him to the same hospital he has been to in the past. I do so humbly and respectfully. The sheriffs, a butch female and a militaristic man, look me over, and I can smell the condescension and disgust of their profession. They also hate me, my own profession. They think I'm useless. They nod to me and say he'll be transported there, but only because that's where they have to bring him as per their district. I think that's bullshit, but I'm not sure.

They leave. Again, I hug the sister after debriefing with her and processing her emotions. The mother never comes out. She looks up at me before I leave and I realize that if I wanted, I could kiss her soon. Perhaps if I requested a meeting next week, I could have sex with her. I envision this. I stare at her coldly on accident. I then smile lukewarm, bid her farewell. I'll meet with her in a week, I say, to keep her informed and plan for the conservatorship process.

I leave. In my car, there's a gust of despair. I feel like crying again, but I realize I can't. I'm an automaton, a failure.

IX

I update Paul. He says I need rest. I look tired. Purple swamps are devouring the islands of my eyes. He looks at me strangely. So does Heidi. I smile unnaturally. But they look fooled. I also update Dr. Weisman. For such a perceptive and erudite psychiatrist, he fails to make note of my disposition and spends forty minutes pontificating on the Axis III basis of all mental illness and how they correlate, a lot of the time, with physical stigmata. He reiterates that I have good genes.

X

I go home. Anaïs calls me. I don't answer. I can't sleep. Everything is slow. I see shadows swirling in the corner of my room. They turn a morose green. I can't distinguish a form but I know that the phenomenon is sentient. I feel terror. I hear mumbling; it's my thoughts. After closing my eyes, they open again in two hours. I close them again, at first tightly, but I force a semblance of rest and obliviousness so the shadows think I'm asleep.

CHAPTER THIRTEEN

I

There comes a time to be honest—and now, I am experiencing that ephemeral moment where clarity returns with a greater degree than ever. In my marrow, I can feel the harrowing. I'm fatigued; I'm animated. I know that I cannot go on forever. What is to be inferred from this, however, is not clear.

I miss my mother. As I float, I recall a silly moment when I was about eight. My mother was ironing and watching a sitcom. I was dead on the hardwood floor, on my stomach, kicking my legs and making fantasy with my toys. She yelled at me because my feet were slamming against the floor; they could have scuffed it, but in hindsight, she was more worried about the distraction of it all. I started crying and looked up, I remember, to see that she was indeterminate, almost pleasant, but in a manner most restrained, as if her face had been jailed. I always remembered it as cruel then. But now I look back, and all I can see is my mother hiding the most joyous and loving of expressions from me. I called her once to appreciate this.

"Hey mom," I said.

"Yeah?" She sounded dry.

"Remember that time I was young and kicking at the floor while you were watching TV? For some reason, I was thinking about it. I remember you yelling, but that you were making the most peculiar face. What was that?"

"Why are you asking?" she said. There was silence. "I don't know, that was a long time ago."

I suppose I also miss my father. However, this was also a new phenomenon. He always smelled like alcohol. However, what I told Lenore was only half true. I spent most of my days hiding from him. For years I hated him. Similarly now, though, my nostalgia conspires to re-educate me on the pretentious uselessness, the childishness of my former milieu of judgments. The pain was real of course. He died before I could develop a mature relationship with him. I was told he had a heart attack when I was seventeen. I don't know if I believe it.

Also, I thought a lot about Lucia. She was my only friend, and I hadn't spoken to her in two weeks. She left me four angry messages and three worried ones. She came to my apartment door once but I didn't answer. Last time I did this, I was a lot younger. She had to come visit me in the hospital. My eyes welled up. I think I love her, but I know that it would never work.

Anaïs—I still hadn't called her either. Just the same, she hadn't called me, having finally stopped trying. It took me a few moments to even find her name in my memory. She was wonderful, but everything was wrong. Unfortunately for my conscience, I had enough experience as a therapist to know that everything was wrong about me perhaps more truthfully. That word again—truth—it didn't signify anything. There is something horribly awry. Anaïs was great; she was patient, tender, affectionate, and understanding. She was also neurotic and insecure, in addition to being whorishly beautiful. How many women would tend to such an intransigent, cold, and dysfunctional man? Valid—it all seemed valid.

10:01 am. I was late for work.

II

I didn't go to the office. If I did that, they would know everything. My phone continued to vibrate. Paul was calling my work phone. He was supposed to provide me with clinical supervision. He had nothing to offer me. I couldn't stand the absurdity of it and the monotony of that morning. I had not the life to act. Now he was calling me on my personal phone. I waited five minutes passed his last call. I dialed Jolie and told her I was in the field visiting Lenore. She instructed me to wait as she fetched Paul. I feigned a weakness of connection.

When I arrived at her house, she wasn't expecting me. I didn't feel like calling her to inform her. A disquiet compelled me to conduct a surprise visit to surmise her more natural habitat.

"What are you doing? Trying to catch me with my other boyfriend?" Her face expressed surprise and anxiety, but she assiduously disguised it with her usual lasciviousness.

"We had an appointment, today."

"No, we didn't. You always call."

There was the slightest tremor to the muscle of her eyebrow. She was trying to read me. She noticed I was different but didn't understand. For a split second, she almost looked scared.

"I know I usually call. Been a busy morning so I just figured I'd stop by to see if you were home."

"I'm always home for you," she said, but then hesitated. "Come on in." Her friendliness was pressured. She was wearing sweat pants and a tight undershirt that accented her petite gut and her breasts. In spite of her maturity and childbearing, she appeared vivacious.

She spoke garrulously as I trailed her. "I'm pretty sure we didn't have an appointment, but then again, I'm not one to remember all the time. I'm sort of flaky... as you know. Want something to drink? —Oh yeah, never mind." She turned back to me. "You sure, though?" She sniggered. "One doesn't hurt, my last therapist would accept water at least, Iosef, and I got the one before her to even try a tamale. I'm sorry my place is a mess, I'm so embarrassed; you're going to think I'm a slob and a bad mother—I'm hardly ever this dirty, it has just been a crazy week, and I've had lots of company—family, friends I mean…" She scurried around cleaning up. As I took a seat on her couch, I noticed her forehead was glistening.

The world possessed a surreal glamor. I took things in slowly. A door opened down the hall. It didn't close, and I heard no steps. I sensed hesitation. I became tense. She turned red.

"Joseph?" Lenore halted and offered me a quick smile. "Come on out, meet my therapist."

Suddenly I heard heavy footsteps, which followed a sporadic moving around of drawers and trinkets on what I imagined to be a dresser. A tall, thin man with slicked salt and pepper hair and a faded tattoo on his neck meandered out timidly. His skin was a dark yellow, and it was leathery; altogether, he looked ill. He was sweating quite obviously, and his pupils were dilated.

"Hey, how you doing?" He made sure to pronounce his syllables carefully. "Nice to meet you. Thanks for trying to help this one, sir."

I smiled and had the premonition that, in conjunction with my blunted listlessness, its nature was disjointed. "Iosef. Nice to meet you."

He lingered. I glanced over at Lenore with more warmth than before. The pupils of her eyes undulated nervously.

"Take care of this one." He laughed and averted his eyes. He looked to say something else but instead nodded and began to make for the door.

"Oh, no, I'm sorry," I said. "Don't leave because of me."

Lenore was swift to answer. "No, he was just visiting, he was actually getting ready to leave before you arrived. He works not too far from here. Sometimes we have coffee and such before he goes to work, before my kids get home, right?" She gave him a loaded look. "We go way back."

I realized that I had never actually met her children.

The man became even more uncomfortable and taciturn. He turned to me, shook my hand, nodded once fervently, and exited with overly attentive movements. His right shoulder bumped into the frame after he seemed to forget how to coordinate the opening of the door and his exiting. He turned around again, smiled, and was gone soon after.

Lenore searched my expression. I didn't laugh, but maybe my face did. She chuckled and shrugged, but it was haunted by strain.

III

For a while, I just sat there as she spoke in heaps about nothing, sweating, her legs opening and closing in cohort with her pupils.

"...Yeah, I've been so busy...I've been doing so much...now I still get up earlier and make the kids breakfast, not just cereal either...but eggs and stuff, but I've already told you that.—And then yeah I take them and...you know how I used to tell you I'd come home and hate myself because I felt so lazy? I hated those days. They were so horrible. I've been working on those worksheets. Well now I don't, hate my days I mean, thanks to journaling. Oh. I make sure to stop by at least two or three spots, you know, like coffee shops or stores or supermarkets, whatever, and I apply for a job too..."

She beamed. Her legs couldn't stop moving. She couldn't stop moving. I caught sight of a whole new droplet forming on her left eyebrow.

"…Anyway, so I've been doing that, and you know, eating better and walking and stuff when I get stressed, like you said, and you know, instead of laying around too, and I've been making my kids dinner too, and I don't know, I just have all this energy, and I can even help them with their homework. — Have you seen the homework these kids have to do?" she exclaimed. "I haven't seen you in so long, either, we've missed our last appointments—well, I've missed our last appointments, I've just been so busy—there's so much to talk about…things aren't perfect, don't get me wrong," she seemed to have started to react to something. "My back has been hurting me again, and I've meant to call you. My neck too. And I have these old bills piling up…"

She laughed again. "Where you been? I've been doing so well, and I wanted you to see. Here, let me show you my journaling." She got up quickly and restlessly and disappeared into her bedroom. When she returned, she was holding a black notebook. Moisture was coming through her thin undershirt around her midsection, quite openly now, where she had been crouching over anxiously.

I accepted the notebook and attempted to make an acknowledgment through the simplest of smiles. Again, her legs began to waft. To me, her breasts appeared swollen, perhaps by her uncomfortable pant.

We made eye contact. Neither of us said anything. I opened the book, averting my eyes from her strange, bothered stare.

"You're too quiet today," she said.

"You're too uncomfortable today," I said.

"You're acting weird."

I held the silence. She stopped moving. I returned to her notebook and started to disinterestedly flip through its pages. The fibrous scrape of each turn only amplified the subsequent moments of wracking disquiet. I heard her exhale; I heard her panting more. She shifted in her seat and crossed her legs away from me.

"I haven't used."

Her voice was obstinate and heavy.

I peeked up, tiredly, bored, and with a sensuousness that was usually alien to me. I felt nothing. I felt like an animal. There was a vacuity to my stomach and chest, a nagging vacuity. But for the first time in years, I felt real life in my masculine corpse.

Her disposition changed. She became powerful with a newfound gravity as she uncrossed her legs to only cross them again in the opposite direction, forcing her body language to engage mine directly. My eyes found her feminine hearth as she did so, and she knew so.

There was a long period of silence, full of exchange.

She arose gradually, and I followed her. She walked towards her bedroom. I mirrored her. The room was dark and pungent; it was cluttered, the bed sheets were wrinkled and askew, and it smelled like sex and smoke.

Neither of us made a sound as we copulated. I fucked her first from the front and then from the back. I thought of Jolie in some moments.

She wouldn't make eye contact with me after that. Her affect was dour, lustful. Only for a moment did she meet my stare. She tried to smile shortly before looking away to take another drag of her smoke. We started again. This time, I focused on the sound of the wetness.

After we had finished, I left without a word. I had her notebook in my hand.

IV

My work phone kept on ringing. I turned it off. The crisis line, which I was carrying, also started to ring. I turned it off.

After sending another call from Paul to voicemail on my personal phone, I made witness of the time before doing the same—it was 4:02 pm. I made a decision. My spirit depreciated before the rumination that I had just so many notes to catch up on.

V

My cognition seemed incommensurable in qualia, suffering from both rapidness and a case of nonexistence. It was 4:49 pm as my body approached its apartment door.

Stickiness and remnants of dampness about my pubic hair paid me bother. When I pulled down my pants, I saw the congealing typical of post-coitus residue left to spoil.

I sat there, somewhere, in the bathroom. There was no time for me.

Everything faded.

All the warmth that I had stolen from others ebbed out.

CHAPTER FOURTEEN

I

I don't remember how I got to the hospital. I woke up and experienced a strike of terror as I realized I was somewhere cold, infected, and foreign. I was in a hospital bed. I had on hospital clothes. People came in. I didn't know them. They had on costumes. I slowly recognized them as medical—I didn't speak, but my sub-verbal vocalizations murmured.

We had an interlocution. I told them that I was looking for certainty and that I should be able to reach this with just a little bit more labor. A social worker came in and made some buzzing noises nonsensically. Suddenly more passion returned to me, and I knew this because I experienced the deepest contempt.

"Did you want to hurt yourself?" he said.

"Of course I did," I said in return. He, of course, didn't comprehend that any being's ultimate aim was to transcend the heterological as part of the tribulations of approaching the auto-logos. Or that I had said this as a joke. His face scrunched up like that of a monkey. He made play at pensiveness, scribbled down something with his dime-store pen, and spoke nonsense. I was a 5150, he said. He was fat, middle-aged, balding, and I hated him.

I laughed and called him a fool and a miserable hack.

I shot up from my lying down position, and after collecting myself from the whirling and tremulous pounding, I leered at him and scoffed in his face.

I shoved him. He appeared afraid. He asked me to desist. I shoved him again after wobbling further from my bed. Others came in. I went to strike one of the blurs, but the choppy nature of my cinematography impaired me. I felt a prick. I went languid again.

Although I never lost my awareness, I unevenly lost what made me care. They transported me to the psych unit without realizing that I had manipulated them into doing so.

And there, I finally got rest—the most unnatural, induced, and harrowing rest where the soul remains awake and in danger within the prison of the saturated brain.

II

Time returned to me eventually but it was not the same. Although I was ultimately only on a 72 hour hold, which included my arrival time, the events of the following day stretched out as if the hours were made from salted taffy and the devil had decided to string out a few bites for the purposes of debauchery and my own imperil.

Upon my arrival, I had been forced to sign an admission that I was being mandated to remain for observation. Really, I had no choice. I felt synthetically groggy. Large orderlies escorted me to my room and informed me that my possessions were safe. They had even taken my shoes. After that, I saw my attending psychiatrist. He introduced himself as Dr. Garagousian. Immediately, I panicked. I knew he would recognize me; perhaps he had already violated my privacy and contacted my boss.

He struck me as bored and self-assured, however, and nothing about him evidenced any need for alarm. If he recognized me, he would have found me more interesting I thought. But the banality of his face convinced me otherwise. He was a tiny, raven-haired man with thick eyebrows and a mask of scorn. He was exactly as I had imagined him to be. After sitting down sharply, he checked his watch and made a stern face.

"Alright, let's get this over with," he said. He motioned impatiently to a social worker, one different from the first, to begin.

"He presented with grossly disorganized behavior, other negative features, and delusions of grandeur, paranoia, and persecution. His thought process was marked by knight's move thinking, and its content is stereotypically metaphorical with a poverty of content. He arrived at the emergency room due to attempted suicide. He ingested about half a bottle of sleeping pills. ER pumped them out. Attacked the medical social worker and was given a benzo shot."

The social worker's voice sounded both disinterested and nervous.

The doctor jotted notes, unmoved. "How'd he get here?"

"His girlfriend and landlord found him with police during a wellness check."

Girlfriend? I didn't have one anymore. Lucia. I writhed.

"Mhm. Ok. Audio hallucinations?"

"None reported, for obvious reasons." He looked at me as a reference. "But he was noted to be responding to internal stimuli."

Dr. Garagousian nodded and scribbled hastily, almost carelessly. "Any medical records?"

"In his file."

The social worker quickly handed the doctor a clipboard, which apparently had numerable sheets of data concerning my physiological and spiritual disposition, unbeknownst to me. He paged through it; the pages made the same fibrous scratching sound so recently implanted in my memory. The doctor looked at me.

"Ok. No compromised liver function and the central depressant should no longer be a huge factor. 2 mL Haloperidol intramuscularly. Anyone checked the integrated system?"

The social worker stared blankly and shrugged.

"Well, this young man, Iosef." The doctor paused and looked at me with new restrained playfulness. "That isn't a common name."

I attempted to signify something, anything, anything empirical, and felt like screaming inaudibly but I couldn't.

"Says here he's Hispanic," the social worker said.

"That's not a Hispanic name." The doctor checked his watch. "Lot of Russians in Argentina, though." He gave me a hard, long look.

He clicked his tongue.

"All right, administer intramuscularly. He has no history, according to these records," he said, haughty and impatient in tone again, "so just do the 2 mL, follow up with 1 mL if agitation persists. I'll follow up tomorrow to assess for discharge."

Garagousian quickly arose, stretched, and made for the door. "Oh." He stopped. "Screenings?"

"Oh! Uh." He took the file back from the doctor and rushed to fumble through it. "No presence of any other substances."

The doctor, without any further acknowledgment, was gone. The social worker arose to follow his lead, suddenly becoming profoundly uncomfortable with my stare. He offered me one final look, which I could return with only a hint of sentience. He assessed me like one does a sequestered dog.

Soon after a nurse arrived. She smiled at me sweetly; she seemed warmer, maternal. She introduced herself, but I couldn't make any special notation of her name. I asked if I was at Mission Hospital. I couldn't remember where Dr. Garagousian worked. "No," she said, calmly, "You're at Valley Presbyterian. They didn't tell you? I'm sorry, honey." She asked me if it was all right to administer some medicine to help me rest and sleep. I gestured affirmatively, and it took all of my being. She nodded, rolled me over, divided my hospital gown, rubbed the meat of my buttock with an alcohol pad, and proceeded to inject me with Haldol. She asked me if I needed anything else and gave me an almost flirty wink of her eye. Completely exhausted, I allowed her to lay me down properly on my bed. Ever debonair, I worked to fix my gown. At least, I pictured myself acting with such dashing. I couldn't be sure as I fell into another troubled and restless prison. But I did hear her chuckle as she skirted out of my room.

III

The Haldol was like a virus disturbing my ability to process information. When I awoke the next day, alone in my sterile room with pale blue walls, everything had a unique slow dripping quality. A different psych nurse, this one much younger, uglier, and boney, dragged herself into my room, stared at me deadly and frivolously, and instructed me that breakfast was being served. I saw her lips move, but her words failed to sync. She administered more medication. By the time I turned around she was gone.

I faded out on an etching on the wall directly ahead of my bed. There were no framed paintings here, or anything else that was tangible. What I gazed upon appeared to be an abstract rendering of a waterfall with mural-like colors of an earthly fashion: browns, ruddy reds, dirtied greens, the such. Staring at it reminded me of vivid dreams, possibly from the night before, but these dreams were broken, they were fragmented and beyond complete recall. I had the grim sensation that they were pertinent, meaningful, but lost. I waited until my tears dried and the pressure, the dread, in my stomach and chest relinquished.

The commissary brimmed with the walking dead. On my way to get my tray, I passed by one middle-aged white man with a flat face, bewildered eyes, and tussled uneven hair. He chewed with his mouth open. He said nothing, but runny eggs and spittle fell from his chin. As I went by him, he mumbled something. I felt in danger.

The next table had a group of people: three young women, and a young man. They appeared higher functioning, curious, nihilistic, sardonic. All of a sudden, I felt an immeasurable shame. I bent my head down and hid my face the best I could. I supposed that the middle-aged man had a severe disorder; he could hurt me. However, these young people, they could *see* me.

"New guy," one of them said, a young girl who couldn't have been older than twenty-two. I ignored her. Out of the corner of my eye, I saw one of them feigning the Thorazine shuffle. When I realized that this was an indication of me, as slow as this realization arrived, I experienced horror.

I couldn't see clearly any longer. I bumped into one of the bolted down round tables in the pale blue room, which was like all other pale blue rooms, except this one was connected to a nurse's station. There were more laughs from afar. An obese Hispanic woman with what appeared to be some sort of genetic issue gawked at me in a manner that I couldn't entirely classify. Her eyes and face were entirely too rotund and inversely correlated. Strange antennae like fleshy growths of about an inch and a half each emerged from the sides of her head in place of ears.

An orderly met me halfway and gave me my food. He helped me find a seat in the corner, away from them all. He seemed to read me and understood my discomfort. I sat down and became obsessed with the plasticity of the cooling powdered eggs. The toast beside it was mashed with butter. For

201

the next thirty minutes, which seemed like an hour, I only touched my food once, although it wasn't to take a bite, but rather to prove its existence. The orange juice was refreshing, however. That I did relish in a single managed sip.

"Aw, he's crying," the young man from the previous group said, taunting me to the snickers of his cohort.

For the rest of the expanse, I sat there and atrophied, as inaudibly as I could, to the blunt indifference of the insane, the bored staff, and the cruel chiding of disinherited youth.

All I could think about was Lucia, my best friend, and how much I wanted to see her at least one more time before I died. That's how I could survive this sickness, this nausea. I thought about her tempestuousness and our joking. I thought of her pain and her rebounding, her stately and bratty authenticity. I thought of her beautiful hair. How I longed to see her, smell her, listen to her voice. I thought about how much I had wasted my life. I hated my career. Indubitably, I truly wanted to help people, but this was marred by failure, by appetite and egoism. I thought about how I could have accomplished something genius and great, and then I thought about how this very thought was the symptom of my disease. I languished, forsaken, dysphoric and impossible—stored away, on time-out in a world within a world, where no matter the level, I was wounded, and ever mortally, by the carelessness and absurdity of no one but myself.

IV

I sat in the corner in the activities room, which shared in the universal décor. The only difference from the commissary area was that this room had a bulletin board that advertised the times for group therapy and activities. Similar to the art stenciled onto the walls, this bulletin board was also a part of it. It was composed of a stretch of wall more darkly colored in order to extenuate chalk scribbles. I believed that it was Sunday. The board offered some number and I had to infer the actual day under the arrest of my faculties.

"Iosef?" A female social worker approached me. She had light olive skin and locks of chestnut hair. "Time for group. We'd love for you to participate."

She gestured softly towards the center of the room. People were already arranging chairs around a table. Three male orderlies with oppressive demeanors lingered near the staff station. They were young, probably in their early twenties, and appeared to be unengaged and hopeful for an altercation.

"Come on," she said, seeming to engage me with some kindness, which made me feel suspicious and strange.

I didn't will the strength to answer verbally although I could in all honesty. After nodding, I followed her to the circle and took a seat. Woozily, I slouched over and awaited the commencement. All the patients from the previous breakfast, on whatever day that was, and a few extras, eventually took their seats. This made me uncomfortable but already everything seemed so distant and blurry.

"Hey everyone, I'm Maria, a therapist here. A few of you have been here for a couple weeks so this may be boring, but allow me to introduce the concept of the group to the newcomers. This is a mental health support group. A lot of us are here because something happened and it was painful." She paused, appreciating the moment. "And you needed some time to rest in a place that was safe for you to do so. We're here to process that." She took another elongated pause. With the word 'process,' I couldn't help but to immediately experience agitation. I shifted in my seat. Astutely, her peripheral vision registered this. "Last week, we discussed resilience and examples of this from our life. Today, let's do another general introduction and start from there."

SHANE SPARKES

Predictable words traveled around the circle. All the patients introduced themselves and mostly said as little as possible. A couple people stated that they suffered from Major Depression and had attempted suicide or had been thinking about it. The youth, including the cruel young man, nonchalantly attested to their Bipolar disorders. One of the younger, more profligate women spoke at length about nothing. She just liked to hear herself chirp. "I do crystal meth too," she said, without due emphasis, somewhere in the middle.

Between these affective disorders there seemed to almost be an unspoken alliance or attraction; they more or less sat closely to one another and within the general radius of Maria. I sat across from them. The rotund, fleshy woman to my left didn't answer the therapist's question; she drooled and generally maintained a bewildered semblance. Every time I glanced over, she met my eyes with too much energy, however, and I would quickly turn my head. I didn't recognize her; I couldn't even begin to surmise her thoughts. She struck me like some quality of mammalian creature, like some form of life lumped into ours for the purposes of taxonomic laziness.

"Schizophrenia, paranoia, see things, went to school, drive but family can drive too, and school nobody flies to…" the odd looking man from breakfast mumbled nonsensically amidst a seemingly random buttress of other words.

Two other patients, equally bizarre in their presentation, avoided eye contact erratically and stayed quiet. All throughout the introduction, I could sense Maria's eyes on me. Eventually, her attention fell upon me directly, and she smiled in wait. The world became shifty again and sticky as if someone hit the slow motion button. I felt like my chest was going to pop.

"Schizoaffective disorder, or so they say," I said.

She allowed the words to satiate. I am sure I slurred. "And how did you join us?"

"I wasn't taking my medication."

She nodded, like a schoolteacher.

"For how long?"

"Over six months."

She paused and prompted me to explain.

"I don't need it."

"How do you reconcile that with your presence here?"

Everyone was staring at me. I stayed silent.

"The med—" she said, but I interrupted.

"The world is cruel."

Her face had contorted almost imperceptibly with the interruption. I watched the subtle reverberations in her throat. They were signs of the nerves of the therapist. Muscle contractions were hard to hide. No one else comprehended this. I did—and it carried special meaning for me. In the following silence, I found a muse.

"I am responsible for so many people at my job. The pressure is immense," I continued. The deadness in my voice was soothing, distant; it overrode the pressure, which eventually faded. More and more, I felt myself. Now I could handle their eyes. The cruel one, his entourage, they watched me, but now without ire; they were children, wide-eyed, awed, frightful, and dumb with wondrous and passive curiosity, feeling so safe so close to their mother.

"How can *I* serve others?"

"Who said you're responsible for them?"

"It's obvious."

Maria frowned.

"What do you do, if you feel comfortable disclosing?"

I glanced at the young adults, the children. "I'm a therapist."

Everyone laughed.

I laughed too, synthetically vertiginous. After steadying my head with my hand, I looked up. I realized my laugh had sounded odd, unnatural. The circle looked off put. "I carry suffering I guess." I paused, searching her expression. Maria's frown remained.

She didn't look so nervous after all. I ceased abruptly.

"Well, it's alright that you're not taking this seriously. But whatever your profession actually is, perhaps you need a new one? Or perhaps there are things in addition to medication that you can do to cope and manage the things that bring you to this place?" She crossed her other leg. "What I mean is, what are your options?"

To die—that is what I thought. To be eaten—that was my conclusion. My face felt slack. I tried to answer, but my jaw moved on the wrong dimension. I experienced a surge of warming as I heard my bones grind, but it dissipated immediately into cool tingles and numb prickles. The medication was fraying my machine. What if it didn't wear off? What if it affected my thinking? Panic returned and my gut clenched. Pressure mounted and forced my heart back into a short, failed race.

"We'll come back to you, Iosef."

"No—no, I was thinking, I'm sorry," I tried my best to force cogency, to not slobber my words, "may I..? I recognize the importance of medication. But I'm afraid of them. They are so new. What are their consequences? Not just side effects, but long-term. How do I know they do not cause brain damage? We always hear about medicines only being discovered to have consequences many decades into their use, when it's too late."

Everyone nodded. "That's a very common and valid fear," Maria said. "I feel anxious and suspicious of medications too when I go to the doctor for health reasons."

"You're right," I said.

She went on about the analogous nature between the necessity of someone taking prescriptions for diabetes or high blood pressure and for mental and/or affective disorders. She beamed, proud of herself. I tried to look captivated, agreeable.

I lost track of the rest of the group meeting. Maria offered me a profound glance at its conclusion, and I acknowledged it. She walked away, inextricably to write her progress note. The orderlies set up a karaoke machine afterward in the same room. The youth made great use of it as I watched from the fraudulent restraints of my invisible, medicinal chains.

Something struck me after the young man sang, jubilant and self-conscious like any vivacious child, and after the young girls indulged in similarly insecure but happy performances of teenage pop songs. These children were not mean spirited; they were frightened and overwhelmed by an indifferent, obtuse, and heavy life, and their barbs were a single reprieve. That wasn't my thought, however; this I already knew, and it was quite vulgar. What struck me was the karaoke itself. In the outside world, normal people karaoke to pretend that they are celebrities. In the mental health world, the patients karaoke to pretend that they are people.

The middle-aged schizophrenic took the microphone and proceeded to attempt the next song, which required him to rhyme in the spirit of gangster hip-hop. To the amazement of his eccentric audience, he performed the song quite well. The entire scene appeared bizarre and disjointed, this older white man with tousled, messy, and greasy hair, with drool on his chin and a wily alien glow to his stare, rapping and jiving to these kids' favorite rapper of the moment—and doing so with unfathomable skill. They cheered him on and laughed rapturously, genuinely. He then became paranoid, glared at them, and dropped the microphone. He started screaming, and the orderlies had to restrain him. They injected him with something. One of the girls started crying and trembling. The young man's eyes welled up too, but he did his best to look menacing and untouched. He quickly started to attend to the girl. As they dragged the yowling, increasingly more limp and silent man away, another orderly, a muscular white male with a tsarist disposition to his soul, lingered nearby, ready. No one moved. He instructed everyone to continue with karaoke amidst the sobs and smell of terror.

The rotund patient embarked on a waddle over to the microphone. She picked it up with extraneous psychomotor retardation and started to mumble monotonously and with no disequilibrium or pause to her flow of white-noise conscious-ness. Only then did the orderly give us space. This phenomenon, for there was no other descriptor, added something bizarre to the atmosphere, but not music, despite the context of bubble gum cheerfulness, light beats, and adolescence.

CHAPTER FIFTEEN

I

Lucia sat vexed beside me in the commissary.

"You have to stop doing this to yourself," she said.

Her cheeks appeared strained, and her demeanor looked generally splenetic and reproachful. She leaned in and stared at me through the upper boundaries of her eyes.

"What the fuck were you thinking? You need to do something. You need to make a change. This is untenable...I'm not going to come here and be all sweet and sorry for you, and all 'oh sweetie, what's a matter,' we're too old for that." She gesticulated sourly. "This was pointless. Again?"

Around us, the other patients, many new ones, were carrying their dinner trays back to the tables around us. Her body language became guarded. After observing the middle-aged schizophrenic with his mange and his coagulant smeared upon his face, she turned towards me again with eyes stern and resolute in their awkward avoidance.

She was scared of them. She was scared of me.

"What, we just going to sit here? What did I even come for then? Why don't you speak?" This last question was accompanied by the dread of a betrothed to the newly paralyzed fiancé. "Move your legs! Please!" the sentence said. "I won't know what to do in life if you cannot!"

"How is school?" I said.

She didn't miss a beat. "Oh, school is school. I'm tired of sitting in class and listening to the same old bullshit. And ...I can't stand all these self-righteous shits discussing privilege. There's this one fucking chickenhead, all made up in makeup, which is ultimately European, is it not?...but with all the indigenous garb...Anyway, if she even knew the history of her allegedly indigenous clothing, she'd also know that the coloring and style are German influenced, and etc., or whatever, but anyway, it is just so apparent that *she* is privileged. She speaks the King's English, perfectly, for God's sake and sits so upright and proper, although she tries to speak so brashly like a *Chicana*." She threw her arms the air, no longer caring about the attention it garnered, but just momentarily. She peered around cautiously before adopting her superciliousness again. "How can these shits, in a university course, who obviously come from decent households and have a middle-class demeanor, and behave so fraudulently with such identity crises, and by the way, who are often mixed or whiter than some white people, speak so judgmentally and pompously about privilege? I mean they have points but we're missing a class analysis." She tossed her hands up one last time. "I'm done. Just get me out of there."

I laughed at her theatrics. She smiled brightly too. "You'll get through it," I said, the tempo and intonation of my words altered, but only minimally.

Her expression changed and she started to cry.

"I don't want you to be different. I don't want you to die." The words were barely intelligible. "I'm sorry...I'm sorry." She gathered herself. A few sniffles attempted to hold the dam, but her efforts were frivolous. She cried again.

We didn't really talk further. After Lucia recovered, we merely sat there and kept each other company. She held my hand and occasionally made a joke. Our eye contact was erratic; however, it was also finally more comfortable but in a manner forlorn in quality. It was like we were sitting together on the curb of an elementary school blacktop, holding hands and decrying, in puerile rebellion, all the brutal facts of life on the precipice of a change.

"I love you," I said. "And I'm sorry. Things will be different now. I will do better. I want to do better."

A bell rang. I wiped away my tears. Somberly, she smiled. She embraced me one last time and promised to keep her phone handy in case I called. I informed her that it was the psychiatrist who would determine my release. We were to meet soon—Dr. Garagousian and I. She asked me if anyone had recognized me, the thought occurring to her immediately after I mentioned this. With a wry and frivolous smirk, I shook my head and indicated in the negative. "You're lucky Anaïs doesn't work here. You still want to try and talk to her, right?" she said. I nodded affirmatively, "Yeah." She sighed in relief and rattled her head to tease me, but this time her reproach intermixed with more than dark humor. I apologized to her again. This time I did not sob. She looked so tired and cynical. We hugged and bid farewell. She walked away.

I waited for her to look back; she didn't.

II

I had been waiting to see the psychiatrist with great trepidation. As per his orders, the nurses continued the regimen of shots to keep the Haldol stable in my blood stream in spite of the fact that I hadn't been agitated. For this reason, I could not overly affect my nerves, although over the past few hours I felt an insatiable urge to move. When I got up to pace, I did so as if my hospital gown was composed of steel mesh. At least I experienced this; I walked stilted and brittle in posture, I believe, but at least I was moving.

Nothing pleased me more than the fantasy of my discharge. As I rebounded between the earthly artwork of the wall and my bed, my mind became quietly rapturous and vulgar in obsessive sequencing and rumination concerning my plans for the next ten years of my life. It escaped me, but I knew that my experience, my intuition, was on the verge of an epiphany. All I had to do was supply for it the time and caregiving requisite for birth. I would secure my release, return to work, and continue the delineation of my first propositions from which I could compose my philosophy.

But would I escape? This question troubled me. What would the psychiatrist note in my affect? What signs were evident beyond my control? If I emphasized the positives, would he observe the consistency of these statements with the rest of me? I mean, I immediately recalled the plethora of instances where I noted the disingenuous manipulation of my clients...I could say I was ready to leave, but would the retardation of my lips and the relative flatness of my spirit inform him of my need for extended hospitalization? This could be the Haldol, I could point this out, but then he could infer my anxiety, and thereby also posit my instability. My thoughts spun on in this way, terribly and intractably labyrinthine.

"Hello. Good evening." Garagousian walked in briskly. He seemed more cheerful but remained short and dry. He made special note that I was pacing. Ergo I abruptly stopped.

"Hello. Good evening," I said.

"How are you?" he said. His eyes were incisive.

"Good." I felt wobbly. Did he see? "I mean, better." Did I slur?

"Mhm." He tapped his pen on his clipboard impatiently. He spent a few seconds flipping through my chart and reading. "So." He gave me one of his long looks. "Who are you?"

"Huh?"

"Exactly." He nodded poignantly with an upturn to his brow. "Who are you?"

"...Iosef Guerrero?"

"And who is Iosef Guerrero?"

"What do you mean?"

He said nothing and stared at me with calculation.

"I'm a..."

I shook my head, dizzy.

"I'm sorry," I said, sounding mechanical. "...I'm a writer."

"Oh?" His attention perked, but his affectation remained laminated by terrible boredom and dismalness.

"Y-yeah."

"What do you write?"

"Oh? Well...I suppose I'm unemployed right now. I write short stories—I bus tables, I was bussing tables."

"What kind of stories? Who is your author?"

Every moment threatened the announcement of my tremulous and feverous sweat. "...I like Anaïs Nin a lot."

"Oh. Ok." He contained his humor. "Why you here?"

"That's general."

"Why are you here?" he said with more authority.

"I have a mood disorder."

"You have more than that."

"I have an affective disorder and a psychotic disorder and when I don't take care of myself..." My eyes lit up, I think—I prayed that they did so in an appropriate manner. "...When I don't take my medications, I mean."

"Good insight." He made a note.

"What's your diagnosis?"

"Schizoaffective disorder."

He nodded again. "Schizoaffective disorder, bipolar type. And what are you going to do when you leave here?"

"Fill my prescriptions. Take my medications every day. Stay away from alcohol and late nights. Turn in some applications, return to work, and work on my writing."

"Sounds good to me. You have a place to go?"

"Yes."

"Where?"

"My girlfriend's."

He stopped writing and peered at me intently from the downturn of his chin. "You have a girlfriend, for real?"

"Yeah, for three years. I want to get married eventually, once I have my life together again. I—"

"Good answer," he said, cutting me off.

I got quiet. I started sweating.

"You have adequate insight. You seem thoughtful, oriented, and are present without gross psychotic features. Any uncomfortable thoughts?"

"No."

"Want to hurt yourself?"

"No."

"Hurt others?"

I shook my head. "No."

"Talk to the social worker for a referral for continuity of care. I'll release you with a 30-day supply. 15 mg of Prozac, 10 mg of Zyprexa—" He stopped. "You have insurance?"

I nodded.

"...10mg of Zyprexa and Depakote, 250mg twice daily. Prozac is the happy pill, Zyprexa controls for uncomfortable thoughts, and the Depakote is to keep you from running all over the place and," he paused to look at the chart. Humor crept into his face. "...And talking about logical transcendence. Well, that's a new one. Take my advice, Iosef. Don't take philosophy so seriously. You know what would happen to the world if we did? Anyway, you might experience dizziness, increases in appetite, tiredness, restlessness, anxiety, and weight gain."

He spoke so fast.

"If you have any extreme or adverse effects I want you to contact urgent care. Sign here."

He finished scribbling and handed me a clipboard with an official paper, one that I recognized in essence, with a multitude of listed medications and an assembly of checked side effects. I signed to acknowledge my informed consent.

"Thank you very much. Have a blessed day. If you have a place to go, since you state that you are no longer a threat to yourself or others, you can discharge whenever."

He arose and walked briskly to the door. "Good luck." I think that was what he said. It was truly indistinguishable, the phrase. And I couldn't tell if it was made with an amicable scoff or shrewd chuckle.

The same sniveling social worker visited me thirty minutes later. He was no more comfortable with me than before. He watched me as I paced for a moment. "You have a place to go?" he said. I nodded yes. "Go ahead and make a call."

Within approximately an hour, I was gone. They returned my things. I didn't have to sign anything else. I was surprised. After changing, an orderly escorted me to the exit with my social worker, and I was gone without further due.

I didn't bother to say goodbye or even to acknowledge anyone as I did so. I just wanted out. Lucia arrived twenty minutes late. Never had I been so happy to wait shivering in the cold.

III

I called in sick the next day, which was Monday. According to my story, I was suffering from seasonal influenza and had required brief hospitalization for pneumonia. Paul sounded grave, angry, masticated. I became worried. "Did he know?" and "Was I in trouble?" were the questions haranguing me without end.

"What's going on?" I said. "I can come in. I swear. I'm sick, but if I need to, I'll be there in thirty minutes." My brain felt a buzz, like an electrical storm from the waning of my Haldol.

"No, no—stay home, rest. Just get better. I'll see you next week. We'll talk then. If I need you, I'll call you."

Lucia missed school for me. She chided me and told me not to preoccupy myself. She tried to hide a disgusted look by turning away as I talked on the phone. My best positing informed me that she wanted me to resign. It was her opinion that I was currently disabled and shouldn't return to such an occupation. She would never come out and say this, though.

The day was exquisitely gorgeous. Chilly as the air seemed there was no visible effluvia to my breath—and the bright yellow rays grazed against the porcelain translucency of my skin, blessing me with an experience of vibrancy extrinsic to my recovering disposition.

We sat there in the sun, mostly in silence, gossiping now and again, although this was mainly her doing, and mostly in regards to whether or not she should reunite with Borges yet another time or if she should look into new adventures. The previous events became a hazy backdrop. Of course, I urged her, and desperately, with groggy passion, to rekindle her love affair with Borges. He was a stupendous man. To my words, my dear Lucia bristled with heedless let-loose.

An ice cream shop was nearby, as was a movie theater. As she spoke, I paid more assiduous attention to each and every passerby. They didn't know me. To them, I was nothing; I was a bench on the side of the street. Everything that had happened signified nothing to them. A little boy stumbled by—he was a toddler and clumsy. He had dark skin and black locks. He gawked at me piercingly as he lagged behind who I assumed to be his mother. He caroused in awkward chubby strides. Momentously, however, this little creature came to a wobbling halt. We made eye contact. And never before have I seen such a pristine and radiant spirit emerge from something so half-done and barely shaped.

At once, I felt rejuvenated. The last trace of the Haldol faded away.

Lucia saw this—and her features adopted the same infectious expression. We all smiled—smiled all around—and what threatened to be a lovely spring day continued on unhindered.

When we departed, Lucia gave me that sort of expression that at once attempted to convey the ubiquitous indifference of the day-to-day, the sentimentalities of camaraderie and an almost familial attachment, and again, a repressed and ineffable despairing and terror at what the future might bring. We hugged tenuously in her car and I pulled myself out from it without climax.

IV

Late that afternoon, I met my bedroom and bathroom again. I could not have cared less at that moment—the memory was already vague and lacking in any forceful constitution. Fragmented images of the vantage point I possessed as I laid in wait of judgment surreptitiously returned—I pictured the strange topsy-turvy angle of my vision as I stared at the black entropic ash flowing upon the ceilings of my bathroom and bedroom beyond it, in addition to the mattress and headboard. The pictorial vanished, and I laughed lowly, quite dry and self-conscious in whimsicality.

I filled my prescriptions. The anti-psychotic was second generation, and there were no longitudinal studies guaranteeing its safety. Again, I played roulette with my mind. But how could

I bring myself to kill the fire within me? What then would be the worth and meaning of my life? —I answered this quite automatically, and in the negative. God had blessed me with his misgivings—or at least, they would be misgivings if I forsook them like an ingrate instead of employing them for their utility.

Sleep cared not to enjoy my company for long that evening. It seemed Death's little mistress and I were still in a piffle tiff. Despite her punishment, after I awoke at approximately a quarter to three in the morning, I returned to my labors. Whenever the mal-effects of fatigue or the medications dared to encroach upon me, the absolute and irreducible pulchritude of the little Saint's smile empowered me to continue on. I would sleep later. I could not refuse God's prompting.

And so that night, I wrote. And I wrote every night after for the remainder of the week to free myself from the shackles, of course also giving myself time for ample rest when I could. My online clinic had yet to be finished and so I dedicated myself to being productive since I was going to be away from work anyway. I cannot say that I wrote with intent; this conscientiousness did plague me. For once again, if what I wrote did not originate, and genuinely, from me, from where did it come? I would curse roughly in these moments and have a tantrum at my desk. Luckily the storm would always pass. I'm sure the medications helped with this, although I was ever fearful that they impacted my potential. I commenced to editing. Soon, it was almost one o'clock in the morning on the Monday next and I had to return to work a little after dawn. Dread colonized my stomach and chest. I gagged. Trusting in chance and the determinism of historical forces, I uploaded the product to my website.

l'art de la thérapie

Psychotherapy is a maieutic art.

Unfortunately, it is one deluded by the 'idolatry of science.' Learning formulae for the reparations or enhancements of human functioning is modern day alchemy. In addition, it is not only the client who changes in this process—the clinician does so as well. Schrodinger uncertainty is not isolated to physics.

This clinic exists, in part, under the shadow of this idea. Psychotherapy is a spiritual relationship; it is also a war of thorny roses and myths. I desired this location so that I could engage in a discourse on the subject and all its subsidiaries.

Too often, although it is all too relevant, the client knows very little about the psychotherapist and the potential variables and dynamics of his or her essence, science, and art. Many reasons exist for this; for instance, we are governed by ethics that dictate boundaries. As necessary as they are, however, they have consequences; they reproduce power relations, invisibly muddle the exchange, and thereby enable miscomprehension and confusion.

For example, if you were in therapy and you witnessed the slightest pinch of your therapist's brow as he or she turned away for the briefest wince, this could have signified 'profundity in process.' Perhaps you considered their following statement in accordance with this perception. Or you might have guessed that you troubled him or her in some inexplicable manner and reacted in whatever way you usually do in those situations. These moments—they mean something, but they often fade without coordinated recognition and definition. Resultantly, they can become the poltergeist of a therapeutic exchange. I am here to write about them—to answer your questions, and to pontificate on my experiences and dilemmas.

You are not my clients, formally; therefore, fewer boundaries exist.

I am also here for you to indulge, and similarly, for myself to indulge as well. A thought, an imagination left unexpressed rebounds, reverberates, redoubles and curdles. There are no faces here; your imagination can feel safe. Hopefully, you will at least be entertained. Comedy is nutritious.

la praxis

In terms of populations, I have worked with people of all ages across a milieu of suffering—bereavement, depression, anxiety, posttraumatic stress, existential angst, etc. Mostly, however, my practice has been focused on those individuals, usually destitute, who suffer from an addiction that is comorbid with socio-psychological misery. They are usually burned beyond recognition. *Et les bénir pour le trouver!*

I do not care to divulge the details of my education. Without a doubt, I can say that it was beneficial. Just the same, I cannot say what *particularly* was beneficial, at least without a second guess. Human beings defy any theoretical manifold. Yet, these manifolds are necessary; they are safety devices and working models. I learned them well. In the end, I synthesized my studies with my experience, and have worked to develop my ability to interact with my clients while observing myself, while monitoring and controlling my intentionality to the best of my ability as to preclude them from my tyranny—which can be a relatively impossible, and at times, pyrrhic obligation. I should not dither here. I'll certainly get lost.

la folie

Psychosis has captured my imagination. Much of my energy will be dedicated to the exploration of the phenomenon. However, what enthralls me to the subject is not the disconnected wonder of the academic, nor the banal pragmatism of the clinician; rather, it is *my experience* that binds me to its immaterial. I think I can free myself if I do this. All modernity points to the fact that self-knowledge can bring freedom.

There is no method of correctly signifying its essence. All language is shared. My experience is not. Thereby, my world is buried by words. Communication is its sepulcher. I can only articulate it in the following fashion: it isn't so much that I *experience* a world; it is more that I suddenly *enter* a different one altogether.

In the first draft of this piece, I wrote about my childhood and my detestable activities as a younger man, about all my first experiences with strange phenomena, my fear and loneliness. I pontificated, gave a narrative. I asked myself, "Why am I this way?" I was digging my grave plot only deeper. It is impossible to *know* me. I've spared you the echo chamber, for isn't this what it is? My awareness means nothing. We are all echo chambers.

My world is charged, changed. Language aside, describing, nevertheless explaining, my experience is also difficult because of the limitations of my memory. However, I can attest to an unnerving sentiment of a relentless vibration, which renders me numb intermittently. Except for the occasional paroxysms of sensations and clarity, this spiritual disposition rules me like Erzsébet Báthory.

I hear noises; I see shadows, wisps, spectral lights. My sense of touch is hypersensitive. On occasion, I feel a shift in pressure on my mattress or a tussling of my hair. Revenants lurk; they threaten to reap. "No, Marquis! It is only your imagination," an inner voice says, only to be stayed by one somehow similar yet monstrous—*"Si, monsieur, but how do you know?"*

To this day, I force myself to ignore the overpowering sensation that something watches me all the time, and sometimes with the intention of preying. To this day, I often experience a nearly inaudible rumble of cognitions, ever so thinly aware that they are mine. They are slow or rapid; however, at times, I *feel* like there *are no thoughts at all*, and even *while I think*. When I speak, sometimes I am unsure of whether or not it is I who is summoning, who is fathoming it. Ask yourself, can you, truly? Can you tell me your thoughts are yours? I am getting lost again! I hope my doubt *infects* you.

My consciousness is meta-consciousness; it is cacophony, made unitary only by my body. There is no salvation, only interminable rebellions, and they are always stalked by the despotism of revolutions. *Nul n'est prophète en son pays!*

Psychosis is a ghost; you cannot see it or really sense it. You do not know it when you are possessed. It takes you, silently. To paraphrase the title of a book rather heuristically, the spirit catches you, and you fall down.

Depression, Anxiety, Psychosis, and Mania—these are the names of my four horsemen. They have loved me with all the violence of the word. They are blood. In part, they construe the reason that I tend to the ill. They are the reason I am here to serve you, dear public.

la guérison

I need to be free. I will be free. Things will be different now. This will be our place to meet, to have group, to restore ourselves in anonymity, our place of restorative justice. This will be our clinic. Together, we will survive and grow.

For once, I am ready to say, 'it is time for my fantasy to die.' We are social beings. I cannot be alone. I cannot be unique. I must become comfortable with meaning. No longer am I a child. I must submit. I must do real work. I must reject my sullenness and take charge.

I have erred terribly. I have betrayed everything. I must make amends.

Never again will I fall down, will I repeat.

Le Marquis de Folie

V

After returning to work that morning, I learned about all the commotion that had transpired since my stay in the hospital. I had been so convinced that I was at fault, that everyone knew, that the crisis had something to do with my transgressions, that my career was over, or at best, that something else unimaginable and unforgivable had happened and I was not there to attend to it and therefore still responsible. But after I met with Paul, who now looked fifty, I was informed that both Weisman and Heidi had quit and that the anteceding and proceeding chaos, which had absolutely nothing to do with me, had overtaken them all.

Wilson had attempted to start a riot at a small protest and the entire foray came to a violent conclusion after he flung himself headlong into an assault on the police. He didn't succeed in starting his revolution, of course; instead, he was almost killed. However, his actions did obtain a small amount of press, for but a fleeting moment, since he had created such a spectacle and because he was once part of the Occupy movement. In the end, though, he was viewed with pathology and not politic. Fellow protesters were quick to explain that he had a mental health diagnosis, hadn't been prescribed medication, and that, as far as they knew, wasn't receiving the appropriate quality of treatment for his needs, which was only yet another sign of the corrupt system. With all the grandiose aplomb of would-be revolutionaries, they declared that his suffering was a fault of our agency.

At any rate, the events hardly warranted widespread attention. After all, I never received a single call about it from Lucia, who often watched the news and knew about these things. I never even caught wind of it myself. Notwithstanding, it warranted attention enough within our little world of mental health.

Blame was thrown around as per the usual. The Inquisition called Dr. Weisman's merit into question first; he rambled on and on with an overproduction of syllables and antiquated Latin phrases before positing that it was the therapist's responsibility to monitor the client regularly for potential decompensation. In short order, he left the company. DMH audited Wilson's file. Paul wrote Heidi up for professional negligence as a liability maneuver. Doubtlessly, she felt betrayed, cornered; she had a nervous breakdown and quit as well, and was now under investigation by the state board for behavioral sciences. He told me all of this with a blunted affect. Paul seemed robbed, vapid. According to him, the higher ups had forced him to do it, to blame her. But I recognized the guilt in his face. Such an affect testified to the daemonic whispers of self-preservation and cowardice. Finally, he cried. I comforted him.

The office was in a state of disingenuous mourning. Rumors prevailed about 'how everyone knew' that Heidi had been emotionally unstable and professionally incompetent all along, and about how it was such a tragedy nevertheless, and about how nobody deserved such a fate, mistakes and obvious shortcomings aside. Weisman was just an unfortunate casualty, people said, but only at first. It didn't take long for the court of Recovery Clinics to hang him in absentia.

I isolated myself in my office. Before starting to catch-up with my notes, I slushed through the contents of my disorganized briefcase, head feeling woozy. I found Lenore's journal. I pulled it out and opened it, finally losing myself in the read. She said lots of things, worked out lots of sentiments, mostly about feeling insecure, negative, and worthless because of her past, feeling ashamed. However, she also wrote about how she was so proud of herself for trying to become the mother that she never had herself, and despite the fact that she had lost custody of her kids. She had relapsed and could not bring herself to tell me. Time and time again, she wrote about how she appreciated my empathy, my warmth, patience, and understanding, about how I wasn't judgmental, and how I was always so courteous and professional.

I finished my work. Once again, I became renowned in the office for helping to pull it all together, for being so bright and hard working, and even while ill with flu. Paul moved up in the company and naturally I inherited his job.

I never saw Lenore again but I thought about her all the time. Napoleon I got conserved and locked away in an institution for mental disease.

Anaïs tried to contact me. We spoke again but in the end my philosophical work was more pertinent. She faded away.

Lucia got married to Borges.

And about two years later I killed myself. I had finally had enough.

www.ingramcontent.com/pod-product-compliance
Lightning Source LLC
Chambersburg PA
CBHW020641260626
47157CB00008B/2852